A NEST OF BROKEN BONES

A NOVEL

JOHN ASHLEY

To all the readers who allow me to continue

chasing this dream, thank you.

I cannot tell you how much it means.

A NEST OF BROKEN BONES

1

Can I get another merlot, please?" Charlotte asked. The heavily tattooed man behind the bar gave her a nod and lifted a wine glass from the rack.

She smiled and thanked him when he handed it to her. Kept her voice sweet and polite despite the worry twisting in her stomach. Charlotte was good at acting. It was her most lethal prowess, and one she always leaned on during these high-stakes outings.

She paid in cash for the wine and tried not to let that fact bother her. The money wasn't a problem. The royalties from her last novel were more than enough to cover a few glasses of wine. No, the problem was that so far tonight, no one else had offered to buy one for her.

The bar was pretty dead. The Sapphire Lounge was rarely ever buzzing with people, but tonight, the pickings were particularly slim. She could have seen it coming. Between the high school football game—a playoff game, at that—and the county fair that had just set up outside of town, most people in Hooper Valley had better things to do this Friday night.

And on the long list of reasons why committing this act here was a bad idea, a lack of targets was far from the top. The Sapphire Lounge was only a twenty-minute drive from where she lived, and "don't shit where you sleep" was a concept she'd always taken to heart.

There were benefits to coming here, too, though; convincing someone to go home with her was a whole lot easier when home was just minutes away. And, tonight, the risk of going back empty-handed was much more threatening than the risk of getting caught.

Malachi would not hold out another sunrise. If she did not provide for him, he would do it himself.

Charlotte lifted the wine glass to her lips and took a long sip, hoping it would calm the sudden shake in her hands. She darted her eyes around the establishment for what must have been the hundredth time tonight, scanning to see if anyone new had filtered in. But she saw only the same crowd as before: two young girls, both blonde and probably related by the looks of it, seated near her at the bar, a man in a suit who looked at least eighty drinking alone on the other side of the bar, a middle-aged couple sharing a plate of fries at one of the tables, and a trio of frat boys in SMU hoodies at the table across from them.

None of them were ideal. None of them came close to deserving what she would do to them. But at this desperate time, the frat boys would have to do.

She took another sip of wine, then adjusted the collar of her maroon blouse. She stood up from the bar and walked straight to their table, making sure—without really having to try—that her hips swayed just so with every step. The boys saw her coming. Their conversation ceased as they watched her approach.

"How's it going?" one of them asked. He was lanky but muscular, with sharp blue eyes and curls of dusty blonde hair poking out from his SMU Mustangs baseball cap.

Charlotte shrugged. "Alright. It'd be going better if I didn't have to drink alone."

At this, one of the other boys—a bulkier fellow with ginger hair and a beard to match—smiled and waved a hand at the table's lone empty chair. "Problem solved, ma'am."

Ma'am. Charlotte knew it was a term of endearment in this part of the country, but it was still grating to hear now that she was in her forties. She didn't let it show, though. She just smiled a little and batted her long eyelashes before reaching for the chair.

"Clint, you're an asshole," the third boy said, jumping up from his seat. "Don't you know you're supposed to pull a lady's chair out for her?"

"Thank you," Charlotte said, lowering herself gracefully into the seat and setting her wine glass down on the table. "So, I take it you..."

Boys, she thought. *Just boys.*

"...men go to SMU?"

"Class of 2027, baby," the tall, blonde fellow said, raising his mug of beer.

"Let me guess," Charlotte said. "Kappa Sig?"

"Hell no," said the ginger. "Lambda Chi."

"Ah."

"How about you?" the third of the students (though Charlotte wondered just how much studying any of them did) asked. He was the most classically good looking of the group, by her approximation, with a perfect jawline and chocolate-colored skin.

"Gamma Phi," Charlotte lied.

"At SMU?" he asked.

"Texas Tech," she lied again. "My name's Laura, by the way." She extended her hand and shook the boy's, letting the touch linger for just a second longer than mere hospitality would have required.

"I'm Zion," he said. "That's Clint sitting next to you, and carrot top there's name is Luke."

Clint lifted his mug and gave her a nod. Luke gave his friend the finger.

"So, what brought you all the way out to Hooper Valley?" Charlotte asked. "Did the bars in Dallas run out of beer?"

"Luke's little cousin plays running back for the Ashville Pirates," Zion said. "They had a playoff game against Hooper Valley tonight."

"Ah," Charlotte said. "I think the bartender's been listening to it on his phone, actually. That game just ended a few minutes ago, though, didn't it?"

"It ended at halftime," Luke grumbled.

"That's when we left anyway," Zion added. "Forty-two to zilch just isn't a score that makes you want to stick around for part two, you know?"

"So, what's the plan now then?" Charlotte asked. She was moving fast, but the clock was ticking. Malachi had been near frenzied when she left. She could only imagine what he was like now.

Zion shrugged. "Head back to campus in a bit, I guess. But one of us is gonna need to sober up some before then."

"Not it," Luke said and took a long swig of his beer.

Clint sighed. "No, don't worry, boys. I know the drill. Somebody's got to be the adult around here."

"Thanks, Pappa," Luke said, grinning. Clint snorted and shook his head.

"Or…" Charlotte said and let her voice trail off. She stared into Zion's eyes for a second, noticing the sudden gleam in them: there because he must have seen the sudden gleam in hers.

"Or what?" he asked.

"Or you could come to my place. I've got a ranch just down the road a bit."

"A ranch, huh?" said Luke.

"A small one," Charlotte replied.

"We wouldn't want to impose on you like that," Zion said. But he looked at her in a way that said that's exactly what he wanted.

Charlotte shrugged. "You wouldn't be. Honestly, I could use the company. I don't mean to trauma dump, but…let's just say tonight hasn't been a very good night for me."

"Breakup?" Zion asked.

"Yeah," Charlotte said. It wasn't true—she hadn't dated anyone since Malachi was born—but that didn't matter tonight.

"Sorry to hear that," Zion said, the lie almost as bald as hers.

"It's whatever. His loss."

"Damn right," Luke said and took a massive swig a beer.

"How are we gonna get there?" Zion asked. "You good to drive?"

"Yeah," Charlotte said. "Only thing is I don't have my car. Not here, I mean. My sister dropped me off."

In reality, her Jeep Grand Cherokee was parked in the back lot. But she couldn't be seen leaving the bar with them. Not in her vehicle, at least. She'd watched all three of them pay their tab with credit cards, which meant tracing them back to this location would be a piece of cake. From there, all it would take was tracking down some patron who happened to see them getting into her car and she'd be caught. Being seen getting into their vehicle wasn't *a lot* better, but it would be easier to explain away if it came to it.

"It's a straight shot," Charlotte said. "And not very far."

"What do you think?" Zion asked, looking at Clint. It must have been his vehicle they came in.

"I mean, yeah," Clint said after thinking about it for only a beat. "I feel fine."

Zion studied his friend for a moment, assessing his sobriety. Then he turned back to Charlotte. "You sure about this?" he asked, a devilish glint in his eyes. "We can get a little rowdy sometimes, you know."

"Oh, I'm counting on it," Charlotte purred.

Five minutes later, they were in the parking lot. Clint hit a button on his key fob, and the headlights flashed on an old, silver BMW parked in the far corner. Charlotte was relieved they hadn't parked in one of the spaces near the door. The back lot would have been even better, but The Sapphire Lounge didn't have outdoor cameras, and no one else was out there to see them. It was as good as she could hope for. It would have to be good enough.

Charlotte pulled her jacket a little tighter as the night breeze stirred. It sent a shiver through her body, even though it wasn't all that chilly. Standing there exposed, with the stars and the moon and whatever existed beyond them looking down on what she did, she felt dual pangs of guilt and despair. How long could she go on like this? She'd inevitably slip up sooner or later. Get caught and locked away. Part of her wanted to. The part so weary and ashamed of what she'd become.

"You alright?" Zion asked as the two of them slid into the BMW's back seat.

"Hmm?" said Charlotte.

"You cold? Hey, Clint, get the heat going up there."

Clint obliged and turned it to full blast. The smell of the heated air and the feeling of it blowing on her face made the queasiness in her stomach even worse, but Charlotte didn't say anything.

"What's the address?" Clint asked. She noticed him holding his phone with the Google Maps app pulled up on the screen.

"Oh, I'll just tell you where to turn," Charlotte said. She couldn't have her address popping up in his Google account if—when—the cops searched it. "It's a straight shot most of the way."

"Alright," Clint said. He sounded a bit perplexed, but he started the car.

Soon they were turning onto the highway. Clint took the turn a little too wide, and the car's front tire veered across the yellow line before he got it straightened back out again. She wondered just how drunk he really was. She closed her eyes and pictured the car swerving right into the path of an oncoming semi. She imagined the collision, the violent force of the impact turning her organs to mush, and the instant, everlasting darkness after it.

Everlasting peace.

But fourteen minutes later when Clint turned the car onto the gravel road leading to her ranch, Charlotte knew it wasn't to be. The queasy, dizzy feeling grew a little stronger, but she pressed it down.

This might not have been the life she wanted, or the one she thought she'd been promised that strange night seven years ago. It might have made death seem like a mercy at times.

But it wasn't just *her* life anymore. She was a mother with a son to care for now.

A son to feed.

2

Luke Howler was used to waking up in places he didn't recognize. Since he first started drinking junior year of high school, there'd been a lot more blackout nights than his parents (and liver) would have liked. So, when his eyes fluttered open and he saw rusted metal rafters on a ceiling high above him instead of the popcorn texture of the ceiling in the frat house where he lived, he wasn't all that surprised.

The real surprise didn't set in until he tried to get up. He grunted and stared down at his feet, finding it hard to process what he was seeing. There was a chain around his ankle.

A fucking *chain*.

Seeing it—feeling the shackle dig into his skin—Luke's heart started to pound. He traced the length of the four-, maybe five-foot-long chain with his eyes and could hardly believe what it was connected to. Found it somehow even more bewildering than the chain itself.

Welded to the chain's final link was a sphere of metal about the size of a medicine ball. Specks of rust dotted the metal's otherwise smooth, black surface. It looked like something pulled straight from the bowels of a medieval dungeon.

The old ball and chain, he could hear his father saying. Except this one wasn't his mother. This was the real deal. And Luke had a sudden, sickening feeling just then when he thought about his mother and father back home in Utah—a feeling he was never going to see them again.

On hands and knees, Luke wretched onto the sawdust-covered ground. It came out watery, tasting bitter and alcoholic. He wiped his mouth with the collar of his t-shirt, then turned his reddened eyes back to the ball and chain.

The ball didn't look all that big, but it was made of solid steel. Maybe even lead for all he knew. Size could be deceiving when it came to objects like that.

He scanned the rest of his surroundings. It looked like he was in some kind of barn. There was a hayloft with a ladder leading up to it at one end, and two large, wooden doors on rollers at the other. Yellow-orange sunlight seeped through the thin cracks along the frame and the larger crack at the center where the two doors met.

A barn. He was chained up in *a barn.* A surge of adrenaline forced him into action, and Luke fell to his knees in front of the ball. He wrapped his thick arms around it, laced his fingers together, and lifted harder than he ever had at the gym. The muscles in his lower back gave a warning shot of pain, but he ignored it and strained even harder.

Maybe a millimeter was all the ball lifted before it slipped from his grasp. It wasn't just the weight of the thing that made it so immovable—though it must have weighed at least 300 pounds; the marble-smooth surface made it almost impossible to grip.

It was hopeless, Luke realized. That's when the fear really dug in its claws. And with it came a feeling Luke knew all too well. His chest tightened; his breaths turned shallow and wheezing. He had an inhaler, had carried it with him since he was a little kid, but he'd left it in Clint's car.

Where that was now in relation to where he was, Luke had no idea. And, come to think of it, where the hell were Clint and Zion? He could vaguely remember the three of them going home with some woman from the bar...Laura? Or Lauren? The details were fuzzy, and the tightness in his chest was all he could focus on.

He was about to sit down, to try and catch his breath again, when he heard a noise behind him: the barn door screeching open.

Luke whirled around, almost tripping over the chain. The crease between the double doors grew to a glowing gap about wingspan wide as the door opened. Then a child stepped through.

Except *was it* a child? On second look, Luke wasn't so sure. The boy's face and freckles and bony limbs all looked like those of a child. Like the features of someone barely old enough to attend school.

But if that was true, then how the hell was he so tall? Luke guessed the boy must have stood five-ten, maybe even close to six feet. He thought at first it might be a trick of perception, like those photos where a boulder was made to look like a mountain or a skyscraper to look like a toy. But that didn't make a lot of sense with him standing so close on level ground.

"Hey!" Luke shouted, then paused to take as deep a breath as he could manage. "Who are you? What is this?" Wide-eyed, Luke pointed dumbly at the ball and chain on his ankle as if it were the most outlandish thing in all the universe.

The kid (*maybe* a kid) didn't answer. All he did was tilt his head a little as he watched Luke. The kind of look a kid might give some interesting bug in the grass. His dark, messy bangs fell in front of his eyes, and he brushed them out of the way with a nonchalant swipe of his hand.

Luke felt a rush of anger then. His fair cheeks turned the same color as his hair, like they always did when he was angry. "Jesus, don't just stand there! Go get help!"

The kid stayed right where he was. He wiped his nose with the back of his hand, then wiped a trail of snot onto his denim overalls. Underneath these, he wore no shirt. Luke could see his ribs on either side of the overalls' bib and his pointy shoulder blades poking out from underneath its straps.

Luke, who had been terrified from the moment he noticed the ball and chain, suddenly felt a different kind of fear creep in. "Who are you?" he asked, more tremble in his voice now than anger.

"My name's Malachi," the boy said, speaking at last. His voice was just as boyish as his appearance but with an edge to it Luke immediately didn't like. "What's yours?"

"Luke. Hey, you're gonna help me, right? I need you to call the police."

"I ain't got a phone," Malachi said in the same dismissive tone of someone telling a panhandler they didn't have any cash in their wallet.

"Can you go get one, please? Or your mom or your dad or... someone?"

"Momma already knows you're here."

Luke felt his stomach turn again. He stammered for a second, his bearded bottom lip quivering a little, before the words began to spill. "What is going on right now? Like, what the hell, man! I want this chain off...NOW!"

"Momma says I'm not supposed to play with my food." Even with Luke screaming at him, the boy's voice stayed measured and steady. "She tried to spank me for it one time."

"Go get your mother," Luke wheezed, finding it even harder to catch his breath now after the exertion of yelling. Though his memory of the previous night was a haze, he had a feeling he knew who this kid's mother was: that cougar bitch from the bar who had invited all three of them back to her place with what had seemed like crystal clear intentions.

"She's not home."

"What about your dad?"

Malachi frowned. The way his dark brown eyes seemed to harden made Luke's skin crawl. For a moment, those features didn't look so boyish anymore. "Daddy isn't home either. Daddy hasn't been home for a long time."

"Alright. Okay." Luke ran his hands through his hair like he always did when he was anxious and tried to keep as calm as possible. "Can you help me then...Malachi? That's what you said your name was, right? Can you please help get out of here?"

Malachi shook his head. "I can't. It'll be lunchtime in a minute."

Luke didn't even know what to say. He just stared at the kid with a bewildered look on his face. Malachi stared back, a strangely unsettling look on his.

"Can you just help me get this chain off?" Luke said. "Maybe find a saw or something. I don't know, just…just help me!"

The boy glanced down at the ball and chain as if just now noticing it, then looked back at Luke. "Okie dokie, artichokey."

He strolled across the barn, and Luke felt a flutter of hope. Maybe this kid had the key. Or at least knew where it was. Luke sat down on his haunches, so eager to have the shackle off his leg, he began to fumble uselessly at it while waiting on the boy.

Malachi knelt beside him, and Luke's nostrils burned a little. The kid smelled like piss and rotten eggs. Crouched like a gargoyle just inches away, his long, undeveloped body looked even more unnatural.

"Do you have a key?" Luke asked. It came out a lot weaker than he thought it would.

"Nope," Malachi said as he wrapped his hands around the shackle. Luke couldn't help but tense a little when the boy's bony fingers touched his flesh.

"What about a hacksaw?"

"Huh-uh." He lifted Luke's leg into the air a few inches, one hand on the shackle and the other clutching his heel.

"Then how are you going to—"

Like this…

The words came from nowhere. Certainly not the boy's unmoving lips. And yet they echoed in Luke's ears at a piercing level of volume.

Before he could react to this disembodied voice, a mushroom cloud of pain bloomed in Luke's lower leg. He watched in utter bewilderment as the shackle slid off his ankle and fell to the sawdust floor with a soft thud, his foot no longer there to stop it. Blood spurted from the ragged stump. Seeing it, Luke felt a scream rise in his throat. But then another sight even more confounding struck him dumb again.

Malachi held the bloody foot he'd ripped from Luke's leg as easy as plucking an apple from the tree. He dangled it over his open mouth so that the stream of blood fell straight down to his lapping tongue. Slowly, his mouth stretched wider. And wider. And *impossibly* wider. Somewhere amidst the shock that engulfed Luke's mind, it reminded him of the way snakes unhinge their jaws to swallow an egg or a rat.

Luke watched as the foot—*his foot*—slipped from the kid's grasp and fell into the chasm. Then came the sound of chewing. Bones crunching, flesh squelching. Luke's stomach heaved, forcing up a burning stream of bile.

The ground began to sway. Luke felt cold all of a sudden: so cold his teeth were chattering. When he looked up at the boy and saw his dark yet gleaming eyes—his pointy, dripping teeth bared in something between a snarl and a smile—the scene was so blurred and swirling that Luke wondered if maybe the whole thing was a dream now fading away.

Surely that was it. This wasn't how he died. It just *couldn't be.*

The kid—or whatever nightmare it was—pounced on him then, limbs flailing, razor teeth gnashing.

It's not real, Luke thought.

It was the last thought that ever crossed his mind.

3

Charlotte rubbed her temples with the tips of her fingers and stared out her kitchen window at a morning that had no right to be so splendid. She'd drank more than she should have last night. Not a lot—only three glasses of wine—but still more than she should have, given the circumstances.

The ghost of a hangover it'd left her with had been the perfect tinder for the ache now blazing in her head. It had flared up the moment she heard that young man's screams coming from the barn.

Sometime soon, she'd have to go clean up the mess. The thought got her head pounding even harder. For better or worse, at least Malachi never left much behind.

What she needed to do right now was cook breakfast. Not for herself; she had no appetite. Not for Malachi either. He'd already eaten. And hopefully, if there was a God, he wouldn't need to eat again for a long while.

There were two others, though, who were probably getting hungry. As much as she wanted to lie down and close her eyes (just to rest, not sleep, lest the nightmares terrorize her), Charlotte owed them a hot meal. They didn't deserve what was going to happen to them. What had already happened to their friend. Three good meals a day was the least she could do until then.

So, Charlotte scrambled eggs in a frying pan and mixed in some cheese, onion, and mushroom even though the smell of it made her queasy. She didn't like eggs herself. Her parents had forced her to eat too many of them as a kid and had turned her against them. Yogurt and a piece of toast was her breakfast of choice, but college boys probably needed something more substantial.

When the eggs had hardened into fluffy yellow flakes, Charlotte scooped them into two separate bowls and put a fork in each one. She filled two glasses with orange juice from the Tropicana carton in her fridge, then set these and the bowls on a wooden serving tray. Then she walked out of the kitchen and headed for the basement door.

There was no telling if the two boys down there were awake yet or not. Charlotte had worked hard to soundproof the basement as much as possible, watching YouTube videos on how to install the sound dampening foam. Even if they were shouting (which, if they were awake, they probably were), she wouldn't be able to hear them from the top of the stairs with the door to the stairway closed.

Getting that door open took some doing. There were two different bolts set into the thick oak, each one with a padlock holding it in place. One of the locks took a key she kept with her at all times. The other was a combination lock that took entering Malachi's birthday to open.

Maybe it was overkill; anyone who woke up in Charlotte Mallory's basement—and plenty had over the years—would have to get the shackle off their leg before they could even make it to the double-locked door. But Charlotte had always been a big believer in better safe than sorry.

She opened the door and stood at the small landing at the top of the basement stairs. She flipped a switch on the wall, and light filled the stairway. From inside the basement, she heard a shuffling sound and the clink of chain links dragging across the concrete floor. Charlotte's heart picked up its rhythm.

"Who's there?" cried a voice from somewhere within the black mouth at the bottom of the stairway. It sounded like Zion, maybe, but Charlotte hardly knew the boys well enough to say for sure.

She glided down the stairs until she reached the second light switch on the wall at their bottom. She hesitated for a moment, then flipped it on.

A trio of long florescent bulbs mounted on the basement's ceiling clicked and started to buzz, illuminating the small space. At the far end of the room, Zion and…Clint—that was the other boy's name, she was pretty sure—sat on the floor and squinted against the sudden brightness.

"Laura?" Zion croaked, recognizing her before his fellow captive. It was a little surprising he remembered the fake name she'd given him considering all the Valium she'd secretly given him as well just an hour later. At first, Charlotte didn't recognize it herself. "What the hell is going on?"

"I brought you breakfast," she said. That didn't answer his question. But he wouldn't believe the real answer anyway. Not until he saw it someday with his own horrified eyes.

Charlotte set the tray down on the floor and gave it a push. Thanks to the little plastic wheels she'd glued to its corners, the tray rolled across the floor with ease, not stopping until it bumped into Clint's shackled left leg. He gawked at it with an expression of sheer confusion. His eyes still looked glazed and lost, like he hadn't been awake for long. She wondered if maybe she'd dosed his drink a little heavier than she should have last night. He was a good bit smaller than the other two, come to think of it.

"Wha…*what?*" Clint looked down at the chain around his leg, followed it with his eyes to the hook in the wall where it was bolted, then gave Charlotte a look that begged for answers.

"I'm sorry." It was the best that she could do. "You need to eat. Both of you."

"Bitch, you need to let us out of here!" Zion said. "That's what needs to fucking happen."

Charlotte didn't flinch. "Can you at least take the dishes off the tray and push it back to me?" she asked. "I won't be able to bring you lunch later if you don't."

Zion glared at the wooden tray with a mix of bewilderment and disdain. Then his jaw tightened, and fire filled his eyes.

Charlotte could have predicted what came next. With one violent sweep of his arm, Zion sent the bowls and glasses flying off the tray. Scrambled eggs went flying into the air and fell like gloppy rain. Both glasses shattered when they hit the cement, splattering orange juice everywhere.

Not a half second too soon, Charlotte noticed Zion pick up the tray and fling it at her. She ducked just in time, heard a helicopter whir as it flew over the top of her head and a sharp clatter a half second later when it hit the stairs.

"There's your tray, bitch!" Zion screamed. "Now get this damn chain off my leg!" Beside him, Clint looked stupefied. He kept staring at the thick shackle locked around his ankle as though it were a hallucination that would disappear if he stared hard enough. If he blinked enough times.

"I'll be back with lunch in a few hours," Charlotte said, her voice still measured. Monotone. "Please make sure your friend isn't hungry first before you throw it too."

Zion kept shouting. Most of it was indiscernible. He'd reached the point of red-faced belligerence that made the string of curses he spat at her difficult to discern.

Charlotte turned away, though part of her thought she should have stood there and heard him out. No doubt that's what she deserved. As she walked back up the stairs, she did something she'd sworn she'd stop doing: she thought about the boys' families. Their mothers and fathers, brothers and sisters (if they had them), and grandparents (if they were still around). It was likely still too early for anyone to have noticed them missing. Too early for anyone who did notice to be *too* alarmed about it, at least. But as the days passed, their worry would grow. Thinking about the lifetime of torment and unanswered prayers she'd sentenced them to—those mothers who surely loved their child as much as she loved hers—made Charlotte feel sick.

"My uncle is a cop, you know," she heard Zion say. The feeling that he'd read her thoughts unnerved Charlotte almost as much as what he'd said. She didn't turn around, but she did pause for a beat near the top of the basement stairs, waiting for her sudden feeling of dizziness to pass.

"He won't ever find you here." The words slipped out before she had a chance to stop them. She'd meant them as self-assurance, but something so cruel should have never been spoken aloud. "I'm sorry," she added. As if it meant anything.

Zion began to scream and curse again, and, next to him, Clint started to wail. Before she broke down crying herself, Charlotte hurried out of the basement, then closed and locked the door.

4

Slumping into his cushioned rolling chair, Sheriff Garcia lifted a Styrofoam cup to his lips, then sighed and set it down on his desk. The girl at the McDonalds had given him decaf. There were probably worse ways to start Monday morning, but that was up there.

A pile of paperwork and a cup full of decaf coffee. Manuel Garcia would have rather been locked in his office with a rabid coyote than these things. He supposed he could send Trisha back to the coffee shop to get him the real deal, but she was a deputy now, not his secretary anymore. He had neglected to fill that role in the four weeks since Trisha Hale passed the academy, and forcing her to continue running his errands now that she was a badge-wearing officer of law wasn't right. Especially since the woman was sharp enough to probably take his job one day. Sooner rather than later, he found himself hoping more and more.

Chasing down bad guys. Protecting the peace and upholding the law. Those were the things he'd always been passionate about. But that was only part of the job. All those years as a kid dreaming of becoming sheriff, or maybe chief of police, he'd never pictured all the paperwork. And press conferences. And bureaucratic bullshit. He guessed it was that way with any career, though: kids who wanted to be engineers probably dreamed about designing amazing inventions, not drafting diagrams and writing code; kids who grew up wanting to be doctors probably never imagined they'd spend as much time attending board meetings and filling out forms as they did saving lives.

It was unavoidable no matter what path in life you took. Bullshit makes the world go 'round. If you want to do anything that actually matters, best be ready to swim through an ocean of it.

At least Manuel had a life raft. A blue-eyed, baby-faced life raft by the name of Deputy Weston Honeycutt. The kid was nothing if not eager to please. So eager to please, it was impossible to tell whether he actually enjoyed doing Manuel's chores for him. Not that Manuel really gave a damn either way. The kid was a greenhorn, and—unlike Deputy Hale, who had won his respect before she ever donned the badge—he needed to earn his stripes.

Manuel was about to pick up the phone on his desk and call him when suddenly it began to ring. He glanced at the number on the caller ID and recognized it. Dallas PD.

"Ah, hell," he muttered. That couldn't be good news. It was, almost certainly, another heaping mound of bullshit waiting for him on the other end of the line. Dutiful to a fault, he picked up the phone anyway.

"Wayne County Sheriff's office. This is Sheriff Garcia speaking."

"Hey, Sheriff, this is Lieutenant Mark Winslow from DPD. You got a minute?"

"Yeah," Manuel said despite the impulse to tell him no. "What can I do for you?"

"I've got a missing persons case I'm looking into. Three college boys from Southern Methodist that were last seen on November 17th. We've talked to some of their friends, and they said the boys left to go watch a football game at Hooper Valley. We checked their credit cards, too, put 'em at a bar in Hooper Valley the night of the 17th. Place called…" Lieutenant Winslow paused. Manuel guessed he was checking his notes. "…The Sapphire Lounge."

Manuel knew of the joint. And, come to think of it, he'd been at the football game too. Hooper Valley had beat the brakes off the Ashville Pirates, and Manuel had stayed until the end, loving every minute of it. He tried to recall if he'd noticed any college-age out-of-towners in the stands, but there'd been so many people there that no one stuck out.

"What vehicle were they driving?" he asked.

"2016 BMW 3 Series. Silver color. The plate is…KLV 427. I can send all the info over in an email, though. I'll get you the boys' names and some recent pictures too."

Manuel scribbled the information down on a pad of paper anyway, crimping the phone against his ear with his shoulder. "Anything else?"

"Yeah, just one more thing. One of them sent a text to one of the friends we talked to at 10:43 p.m., which is shortly after they paid their tabs at The Sapphire Lounge. He said, quote, 'Bro, some MILF at this bar wants us to run a train on her.' Are you, uh…you familiar with the terminology, Sheriff?"

"I get the idea," Manuel said.

"Might be nothing. But whoever he was talking about could've been the last person to see them. If she's even real, that is."

"I'll send a deputy down to The Sapphire Lounge. Figure out who was working that night and see if I can get 'em in for a talk. And I'll get an APB out on that vehicle too."

"Thank you, Sheriff. I'll keep you in the loop if anything else comes up."

Manuel hung up the phone. He drummed his fingers against the desk for a minute and let his vision go out of focus. Then he picked up the phone again and dialed a number he knew by heart.

"What's up, Manny?" a gritty voice said after a couple of rings. It was a smoker's voice, getting worse by the year, but Manuel had given up trying to convince Detective Garret Stark to give up the habit.

"Hey, you remember that MPC you worked a couple years ago?" he asked. "The young, short-haired girl out of Dawson. Can't remember her name. Becka something."

"Becka Green. And I'm still working it, technically. We never closed that case."

"Remind me what her last known location was again."

"The Sapphire Lounge," Detective Stark said. "Dave Johnson was running the bar that night. Said she came in about 9:30. He didn't notice her leave, but he guessed it must have been sometime around eleven."

"Yeah," Manuel said, drumming his fingers against the desk again. "That's what I thought."

"How come you want to know about the Green case?"

"Just got a call from DPD. They got three boys from SMU been missing sixteen days. I'll let you guess what their last known location was."

"No shit?"

"Uh-huh."

"You don't think they're connected, do you?" The detective's tone told Manuel what he thought already. It made sense, too; the kind of psychopaths that would scoop up a 90-pound girl with a pixie cut didn't usually decide to target a trio of strapping young college boys the next go-around. And that's assuming any of them ever crossed paths with said psychopath in the first place. They'd never found Becka Green's body. For all anyone knew, she and the SMU students both could have just cut ties and run away to some new life, their last known stop at The Sapphire Lounge being only a coincidence.

"Probably not," Manuel said. "But I hate coincidences."

"I know what you mean. Kind of wish I could take a look at it myself."

"It's Dallas's case. But they're getting anxious already if they're calling here for help. They might get desperate enough to loop HVPD in too."

"Yeah, right," Detective Stark said. "You know how that asshat over at Dallas feels about Chief Renly."

Manuel knew the basics. Chief Hannah Renly of Hooper Valley PD and Chief Isach Adams of Dallas PD used to work together in DPD's narcotics unit until a falling out between them that was bad enough for Renly to transfer. Rumor was they'd been sleeping together and the whole thing was a lover's quarrel. It was unproven but not hard to believe; a male and female cop *not* sleeping together would've been the bigger story.

"I'll keep you updated," Manuel said.

"I appreciate it, Manny."

Manuel hung up the phone. He sat there for a while, staring at the stack of papers on his desk but not really seeing them anymore. These were the moments when all the paperwork—all the bullshit—didn't seem so bad. The moments when his ears perked up and his bloodhound nose caught a whiff of a trail.

5

BEFORE

Charlotte pressed her fingers into her ears hard enough to hurt and stared at the glowing, blank Word Processor page on her laptop. Even with them nearly buried to her eardrums, she could still hear his shrill screams.

It wasn't just the noise that bothered her, though that alone was plenty piercing and distracting. But the nurturing, protective instincts that flared inside her each time she heard him wail was even worse.

If fixing it were possible, she would have. But the kid wasn't hungry—he'd practically slapped the bottle away—and his diaper was clean. Holding him hadn't helped either. That seemed to only make things worse.

It had been going on like this all day. She'd have to get him to the doctor if it persisted, but Charlotte figured teething was most likely the issue. Little Malachi's molars were finally starting to come in. Just a month short of two years old, he was a bit behind the curve on that particular developmental milestone.

That was the only one he was behind on, though. The "little" in "little Malachi"—one of her numerous pet names for him—was a relative term. At thirty-eight pounds and forty-one inches already, he was probably the largest two-year-old she'd ever seen. And still growing like a weed.

Another blaring scream echoed in her skull. It was a good thing she didn't have any neighbors, Charlotte thought. They'd probably wonder what she was doing to the poor baby.

On her laptop screen, the cursor kept blinking away. It looked a little alarming there on the empty page with not a finished word around it. Like a light blinking on a time bomb.

Her laptop wouldn't blow up if she didn't finish the additional material for *Destiny's Desire* by next Friday. But her editor probably would.

Sighing, not wanting to do it, Charlotte fished her phone out of her jeans pocket and dialed Deborah Vickers's number. The phone rang for a while. Charlotte started to wonder if she'd pick up and partly—for her sake—hoped she wouldn't. Deborah Vickers was getting on in years and poor in health. That she was the only friend in all of Hooper Valley—all the world, really—whom Charlotte could call for help only made her feel worse about the situation.

Then, the ringing stopped, interrupted by a rustle of sound. "Hello?"

"Hey, Deborah, how are you—"

Another scream coming from Malachi's playpen in the living room cut her off.

"Oh, my goodness," Deborah said. "That is not a happy baby, is it?"

"No, he is not."

"Poor little fellow. Let me put some proper clothes on, and I'll be right over."

"Thank you, Deborah," Charlotte said, grateful for the offer and even more grateful that Mrs. Vickers hadn't made her ask. It was one of the many things she appreciated about the woman. "You're a saint."

"Oh, pish posh. You just hold steady, dear. We'll see if Granny Vickers can't get that boy cheered up."

Charlotte thanked her again before ending the call, then slumped back in her office chair. An afternoon in a quiet coffee shop while Deborah tended to Malachi would be enough to bang out the majority of the chapter she owed her editor. And even with its deadline looming, the thought of spending the rest of the day in relative silence save for the low din of conversation and baristas brewing drinks seemed like a little slice of Heaven.

Another shrill scream from the living room made Charlotte wince. Then she cringed a little when she thought of Deborah, probably already on the way in her old Lincoln Town Car. Neither the car nor its driver really should have been on the road anymore, but good luck telling that to Deborah Vickers. And while she was still spry enough to care for a toddler on occasion, Charlotte supposed, she was just barely so.

What am I getting that poor old woman into? Charlotte thought, feeling strangely disquieted all of a sudden for reasons she couldn't diagnose.

The five hours Charlotte spent writing at Java Junction had been some of the most productive of her entire career. The words had come like water from a broken levee the moment she'd settled into the peaceful corner booth.

She'd told Deborah she would be home in three hours, four at the latest, but she just couldn't bring herself to stop. Make hay while sun's shining, strike while the iron's hot, and all that. And pushing through that one extra hour had allowed her to completely finish the new chapter for *Destiny's Desire*.

Winding down at last now that the chapter was finished, it felt like coming down from her favorite kind of high. But now that the gears in her mind were slowing to a halt, Malachi—and Deborah there alone with him—was all she could think about.

Charlotte picked up her phone and dialed Deborah's number. It rang and rang and rang. Then it went to voicemail. A stab of worry made Charlotte frown. Though it wouldn't be the first time Deborah had let her phone die, Charlotte reminded herself. That was almost certainly the answer. Or maybe Malachi was still screaming so loud the poor woman never heard it ring. She hoped that wasn't the case, but she would have taken it over...well, *worse* alternatives.

Either way, Charlotte was suddenly more eager than ever to get home. She stuffed her laptop and notebook into a floral-patterned laptop bag and swung the strap over her shoulder.

"Have a nice night," the curly-haired barista told her as she headed for the door. Without meaning to, without ever thinking about it, Charlotte ignored her.

Soon she was in her Jeep and driving down Highway 97. Her house was just a twenty-minute drive from the coffee shop, fifteen if she sped, which she was already doing. She tried again to call Deborah using her car's hands-free feature. Again, no answer.

Charlotte's mouth felt dry even though her bladder felt like it was going to burst. Like her body couldn't make up its mind whether it was hydrated or not. She needed to focus on where she was going. The growl of the rumble strip as her right tire veered across it drove this message home. Whatever the reason why Deborah wasn't answering her phone—and it was most likely nothing—making Malachi an orphan on the way home wouldn't help. An orphan herself for most of her life, she knew all too well what she'd be sentencing him to.

By the time Charlotte pulled off the highway and onto the dirt road leading up to the 120- acre ranch she'd purchased almost as soon as the advance for *Tempting the Devil* hit the bank, the sixteen minutes it had taken felt like the longest drive she'd been on in ages.

Deborah's car was still there in the driveway. That was a good sign. It meant she hadn't rushed Malachi off to the hospital at least. Charlotte pulled up beside it and put her Jeep into park.

The lights in the house were still on. All the curtains were drawn, so she couldn't see inside, but she could see the yellow glow coming through them. Charlotte hurried up the porch and punched her code into the lock's keypad, swearing under her breath when her shaking fingers hit the wrong number and she had to start over. Her instincts were blaring now like air raid sirens. She'd heard before of a mother's intuition, but she'd never experienced it herself until now.

When the lock's digital screen turned green and the bolt retracted, Charlotte flung open the door. At first, she saw nothing out of sorts. Just the long entryway into her home with the chandelier on the ceiling lighting it in a golden glow. But another step into the house was when it struck her. Not the sight of something, but the smell. It was faint yet unmistakable: an acidic, rusted-penny scent that filled the entire space.

"Malachi!" Charlotte screamed, barreling down the hallway toward the living room at its end. Terror seized her like an electric current. It seemed for a moment she might faint mid-stride. But Charlotte fought through it, grasping at the arched wall to steady herself as she entered the living room.

The first thing she noticed—the first thing anyone who entered that room would have noticed—was all the blood. It dripped from the cushions of her cream white couch and pooled on the hardwood floor in puddles big enough to splash in.

Splashing. Surely that's not what she was hearing. Surely it wasn't what she was seeing. In her hallucination—for Charlotte had already decided that's what it had to be—she saw Malachi sitting on the floor wearing nothing but his diaper. The pool of blood all around him was deep enough to cover the bottoms of his pudgy, out-stretched legs. Deep enough to make that sticky, awful splashing sound each time he giggled and smacked his hands into it like playing in the bathtub.

Charlotte rushed to him and scooped him up in her arms, still unconvinced the blood coating his body wasn't his. But she'd already seen its source from the corner of her eye.

Deborah Vickers was lying on the floor beside the couch. Her dress was hiked up over her face. Her exposed stomach was torn open, her round midsection now a grisly, red crater. Broken ribs stuck out from its rim. Organs and entrails littered the floor around it, and Deborah's glazed eyes stared up at the ceiling fan above where she lay.

Seeing her there, a jolt of ice-cold fear surged through Charlotte's veins. Someone had done this. Someone who could still be in the house.

She hoisted Malachi over her shoulder, struggling a little at first. God, he'd got so heavy already. Then she sprinted for her bedroom door.

She threw Malachi down on the bed, oblivious to the stains it would leave on her silk comforter, then closed and locked the door. She flung open the drawer of her nightstand and pulled a hard plastic case out of it. It was locked—a necessity with such a young child in the house but a nauseating obstacle at the moment. After a few tense seconds, she managed to punch in the combination and retrieved what used to be her foster father's Glock 19 from the case. She remembered what he'd taught her and racked the slide. Once it was chambered, she took out her phone and dialed 911.

"9-1-1, do you need police, fire, or medical assistance?" a male voice said.

"Police! And medical!"

"What's the address of your emergency, ma'am?"

"It's 100—"

A sucking sound cut her off. Charlotte turned her attention to the foot of the bed where Malachi was sitting and saw him with his thumb in his mouth. A bubbly mix of blood and saliva pooled around his lips as he sucked away at the digit.

"Malachi!" Charlotte said as she pulled his hand away from his mouth. She realized then that she was pointing the gun right at his head. She died a little inside and set it down on the nightstand out of his reach.

"Ma'am, what's the address of your emergency?" said the voice on the call she'd momentarily forgotten about.

"It's 100 Hawkins Road, just south of town. Hurry! Someone broke into my house and. . . oh, God! They tore her apart!"

"Tore who apart, ma'am?"

"Her name's Deborah. Deborah Vickers. She was baby-sitting my son, and I came home, and...oh, please hurry!"

"I've got officers en route. Get somewhere safe, behind a locked door if you can, and stay on the line. Okay?"

"Okay," Charlotte said and took a ragged breath. "Okay."

On the bed, Malachi clapped his bloodstained hands, spread his lips in a snaggle-toothed smile, and started to laugh.

6

BEFORE

Sheriff Garcia took a deep breath of the autumn night air and chewed at the corner of his lip. Thirty-seven years wearing a badge and the job still managed to surprise him. Not even the largely rural Wayne County was immune to the shocking depths of human depravity.

Someone had gutted Deborah Vickers like a fish. Right there on the living room floor of Charlotte Mallory's home while her two-year-old son looked on. Sheriff Garcia had met Deborah before in passing. On a few occasions, he'd bought vegetables from the roadside stand she and her husband set up near the Hooper Valley municipal build-ing. And everyone in the area knew of Charlotte Mallory, the big-shot romance writer. Manuel didn't care much for her books, thought of them as pornos in the written form, but neither she nor Mrs. Vickers seemed like the type to have enemies. Not dangerous ones anyway.

Yet, depraved as it was, it wasn't even the murder itself that bothered Manuel most. It was all the rest of the details that kept surfacing one by one as they examined the crime scene. Starting with the fact that there was zero sign of forced entry. No broken windows, no busted locks. Stranger still, Charlotte had told him that the door was locked when she arrived. Either it'd been unlocked when the killer got there, or Mrs. Vickers had let him in. And, either way, someone had locked it again.

Next, there was the blood spatter. They'd identified the prints of Charlotte's sandals in the lagoon of blood that covered the living room floor, and the barefoot prints of her boy, too. But no others. The killer could have avoided leaving prints if he'd covered his shoes in plastic, but your run-of-the-mill psychos didn't usually think of that. That was more the trademark of a professional. Which, given the victim, made the motive hard to imagine.

Money was one obvious motive. It was no secret that Charlotte Mallory had a lot of it. But not a single item in the home was missing. Her jewelry was still in its cases. The expensive art littered throughout the home was left undisturbed. And taking the child ransom had obviously not been their goal either; he'd been left without a hair on his head touched.

"What do you think, Sheriff?" Deputy Rodgers asked, strolling up to the squad car Manuel leaned against.

"I think we'd better hope those state boys and their CSI geeks can find a print. Or a hair or something," Manuel said.

All the way out here, the odds that anyone had seen anything were slim. He'd been hopeful that Ms. Mallory would have security cameras on the property, but no dice.

"What about the woman and her kid? You know if they've got anywhere to stay?"

"She says she's got a sister that lives in town. I'll have you give 'em a ride here in a bit. She's in no state to drive. But I want to talk to her again first, before we let her go."

Who he actually wanted to talk to was the kid. He'd already got all he was going to get out of Ms. Mallory. By the time she'd shown up, everything had already happened. But the kid...he'd presumably seen it all. What he remembered, what he was capable of communicating at such a young age, was anyone's guess. But Manuel was eager to find out.

That meant approaching a momma bear who was still in full defensive mode. Not usually a very smart idea, but Sheriff Garcia didn't consider himself a very smart man. At least not when it came to acts of self-preservation.

Ms. Mallory was sitting on the top step of her front porch, her son right next to her about as close as she could get him. She watched the sheriff approach, but her eyes didn't seem like they really saw what they were looking at. He could only imagine the woman's shock. The condition of the body had made even his hardened stomach turn; it looked like the poor old woman had been torn apart by a lion.

"Ms. Mallory," Manuel said. "How are you holding up?"

She shrugged. With the flashing red and blue lights reflecting off her pallid face, she looked ghostly. Like a character on a haunted hayride.

"I'm gonna have Deputy Rodgers take you to your sister's here in a minute. Will that work?"

"Yes," Charlotte said.

"But first, I was hoping I could talk with your boy."

Charlotte eyed him suspiciously. "He's been through a lot, Sheriff."

"I know, ma'am. I won't be long."

"And he's barely talking. I mean, he isn't even speaking full sentences yet."

"I kind of figured that too. I'd like to try anyway, if it's alright with you."

She took a while to think about it, then exhaled and said, "Okay. Just please don't ask him anything upsetting."

"Of course not," Manuel said.

Nuzzled against the woman's lap, the dark-haired boy looked half asleep. But when she rubbed his shoulders, he yawned and rubbed his eyes.

"Malachi," Charlotte whispered. "This policeman needs to ask you a few questions. Okay?"

Malachi looked up at the uniformed man standing over him, his sleepy expression twisting into mild confusion. "Hi there," Manuel said, kneeling so that he was on the kid's level. "My name's Manuel. What's your name?"

Malachi just stared at him.

"Can you tell the policeman your name?" Charlotte asked. Malachi shook his head.

This was pointless, Manuel could already tell. But he wouldn't be doing his job if he didn't try. "Do you remember the nice old lady that was taking care of you today? Her name was Deborah Vickers."

"Mish Debba," Malachi proclaimed, scratching flakes of dried blood from his scalp with equally grubby fingers. Manuel could see in her eyes how eager Mom was to get him away from here, to get him in a bath and clean clothes and hold him in her arms the entire rest of the night. Hell, it might be months before she let go of him again.

"Did you see what happened to her, Malachi?" The kid didn't answer this, didn't act like he'd even heard it, so Manuel asked a different question. "Did a man come into the house before your mom got home?'

"Hmmmmmmmm," Malachi said, drawing out the word until he must have been nearly out of oxygen. "Nope."

Manuel wasn't sure how much stock he could put in this. Probably not much. "Are you sure?"

"Mmm-hmmm," Malachi said, and gave two sweeping nods of his head.

"Who hurt Miss Deborah then?" But Malachi had turned his attention to one of the squad cars in the driveway, his eyes settling on its colorful lights. "Who hurt Miss Deborah, Malachi?"

"I dids it."

Though no part of him believed for an instant what the kid had just said, a chill slivered down Manuel's spine anyway.

"I'm sorry, Sheriff," Charlotte said.

"No worries, ma'am."

"If it's alright, I'd like to leave now."

Manuel nodded and motioned Deputy Rodgers over. "Deputy Rodgers here will take you to your sister's," he told Charlotte. "I'm gonna have him post up outside her house for the night too."

"Thank you," Charlotte said. She sounded stunned. Looked it too. Not her boy, though. The short nap he'd taken in Mom's lap seemed to have reenergized him; now, he was twisting like a snake, trying to wriggle free of her grasp.

"Here, I can take him, ma'am," Deputy Rodgers said, walking up with his arms outstretched. Manuel could have told him how that was going to go. Charlotte stood hastily and swept the boy up into her arms, casting Deputy Rodgers a briefly defensive look.

"I've got him, thank you. You just lead the way."

But she did struggle a little with him, Manuel noticed. Especially with the boy still wriggling and writhing. Goodness, he was big for his age. With so much else going on, it hadn't caught Manuel's attention until now. He could have sworn he heard Charlotte say the boy was two years old. But that probably wasn't right. The kid looked three at least, maybe four.

Manuel watched her help Malachi into the back seat of Deputy Rodgers's car. She got in beside him once he was buckled in, and Rodgers drove them away. Manuel stared at the taillights and the cloud of dirt road dust behind them until the car turned onto the highway. Then, unexpectedly, he thought of the body still lying on Charlotte Mallory's floor. The way the woman's entire abdomen had been torn open. Ripped apart.

Sheriff Garcia was not a man who spooked easily. But when a gust of cold November wind whined through the trees behind the house and chilled his skin, he developed a case of the frights that persisted the rest of the night.

7

Charlotte filled a pitcher with bathwater and tipped it over Malachi's head. He clenched his eyes shut as the streams of water and shampoo suds washed down his face.

He had to sit up to fit in the tub, and, even then, he couldn't stretch his lanky legs out all the way. Charlotte wasn't sure what she'd do if he kept growing at his current rate. Install a larger tub, she supposed. It was such a trivial solution to a problem so much bigger than bath time that the idea of it made her laugh.

"What's funny, Momma?" Malachi asked when he got done wiping the water from his eyes.

"Nothing, baby," she said. Nothing at all. Thinking of the future, *his* future, was truly no laughing matter. What was he to become, this miracle child of hers? What kind of life could someone like him possibly live besides one of pain and sorrow?

A life spent with her was the answer, for as long as she lived, at least. She could continue to hide him away on this ranch until he was a grown man and she a gray-haired woman. No one would ever know; as far as anyone else in the world knew, her son had died four years ago.

Despite all the novels to her name, convincing everyone that this fiction was true had been her greatest feat of storytelling so far. There'd been no room for plot holes or loose threads in that story. And suspicious lawmen were a whole lot more discerning than the average romance reader.

It wasn't all roses, though, hiding him away like this. She could only imagine the toll it took on him.

"Momma, why don't I have any friends?" Malachi had asked her one morning while they sat at the kitchen table, working on addition and subtraction. That'd been nearly two months ago, but the words still came back to her now and then to rip open her heart anew.

Right now, at least, he seemed happy. Most times, he was as happy and normal as any child his age. At times like this, it was so easy for her to pretend, to forget all the darkness and haunting questions that plagued her mind. Scrubbing his back with a washrag while Malachi played with his bath toys, she felt happy and normal too, if but for a moment. Aside from caring for him, moments like these were all that she still lived for.

Charlotte grabbed a towel from the bathroom cabinet. She was about to help Malachi up out of the tub when she spotted a fleck of dirt she must have missed, hidden away behind his left ear. She grabbed her wet washrag and looked closer.

It wasn't dirt. The slight tinge of red to its black-brown color gave it away. Charlotte felt her stomach twist. It had been over two weeks since Malachi last fed. At least a dozen baths between now and then. Had she really missed this spot all those times?

She must have. She didn't want to think about the alternative—that Malachi had slipped away while she napped this afternoon and gone hunting on his own.

The blood looked old. Definitely older than a day. With a quick wipe of the cloth, it was gone. She tried to wipe it from her mind too, but that was not nearly as easy.

Something so little was all it took to shatter the illusion. There was always some reminder to bring her crashing back down to…

Reality? Could she call it reality when it was all so nightmarish and absurd? When every day felt like a bad dream she'd surely wake from any moment.

She helped Malachi into his PJs, then tucked him into his bed. A full-size bed, it, too, was already getting too small for him. She wondered at what point he'd stop growing, then wondered if he ever would.

"I love you, Momma," he said as she turned out the lights. His voice was sleepy. Soft and warm as melted sugar.

Just then, for a fleeting moment, Charlotte captured that feeling again.

8

Sheriff Garcia stared at the name on his computer screen in stunned disbelief. He hadn't recognized the first two names in the email from Lieutenant Winslow of DPD. Luke Howler and Clint Davis weren't anyone he knew from Adam.

But he did recognize the third name. Zion Brooks. Unless there was another one of them that lived in Dallas, it was his nephew.

There was an attachment at the bottom of the message. He clicked on it once, then several times rapidly, but he couldn't get it to open. The department had switched email providers last month—security reasons, is what the IT guys had said when they asked him to sign off on it—and he hadn't been able to get anything to work right since.

"Well, shit," he muttered, then leaned toward his open office door and shouted, "Hey, Reed! Come in here real quick."

"What's up, boss?" Deputy Trent Reed asked, stepping inside.

Deputy Reed had a kind of weaselly look about him, with narrow features and thin ginger hair. It had made Manuel a bit unsure of him when he first joined the department. But he had proven himself to be a fine officer.

Right now, all Manuel needed him to be was half decent with computers. "I'm trying to open this attachment, but the damn thing won't work."

"You got to right click on 'em now," Deputy Reed said. He circled around the desk and reached for the mouse.

"I know how to right click, son," Manuel said, pulling the mouse away from him. He recentered it again on the attachment and clicked the right button. A dropdown menu opened, with the option "open file" at the top. Manuel clicked it.

Zion's was the first picture he saw. "Damn it," he swore under his breath. Some part of him had still been holding out hope that maybe there was another Zion Brooks from Dallas. But that ship had sailed now. It must have been seven, maybe eight years since he'd seen Marissa's oldest boy. His sister didn't have much to do with him these days. Didn't have *anything* to do with him, really. It struck him then that she hadn't even reached out to tell him the boy was missing.

But despite not seeing Zion since he was in middle school, Manuel recognized his picture without a doubt. Half Black from his dad's side and half Mexican from his mother's, the boy had a unique look about him. And the little scar on the side of his chin sealed the deal. Manuel had been there at the family barbecue twelve or thirteen years ago to see the tumble down the porch that caused it. That had been before his relationship with Marissa started to circle the drain.

"Something wrong, Sheriff?" Deputy Reed asked.

"My nephew's gone missing," Manuel replied, still staring at the picture on his screen. "Been missing sixteen days now."

"No kidding?" Deputy Reed said. Then, "I didn't know you had a nephew."

I probably don't anymore, Manuel thought.

The well-known idea that you have forty-eight hours to find a missing person before the odds of ever finding them plummeted was a bit of an oversimplification. Runaways accounted for the vast majority of missing persons cases, and it wasn't uncommon at all for them to stay gone longer than two days before they were found or returned on their own.

But Zion and the two boys he'd gone missing with weren't runaways. It didn't seem very likely at least; all three of them presumably paid good money to attend SMU, and Manuel was pretty sure he remembered seeing somewhere on social media recently where Zion had a girlfriend. If disappearing sixteen days (and counting) hadn't been their choice, that didn't leave a lot of good possibilities.

"Think you can hold down the fort for a bit?" Manuel asked.

"Yeah, sure," Deputy Reed said. "Where you headed?"

"Going to a bar," Manuel said. Then he grabbed his duty jacket off the hook on his office wall and headed out the door.

Manuel, who had once spent the better part of his days and nights in joints like The Sapphire Lounge, found the sharp scent of wood polish and alcohol fumes when he opened the door strangely haunting. Such watering holes had been his Garden of Eden in his younger years. Just like Adam and Eve in the story, he, too, had lost control of his temptations and ended up barred from paradise. There weren't any angels with fiery swords guarding the bars he used to frequent, but there was a chip in his left pocket with the words "Five Years" engraved across it. And he had no intention of giving it back.

Manuel chose a stool near the center of the horseshoe-shaped bar and sat down. It didn't take long for the barkeep to notice him.

"What can I do you for, Sheriff?" Jack Godfrey asked. He popped the cap off a Pilsner and set it down in front of a thin old man in a flannel shirt a couple seats down before returning his attention to Manuel. "You ain't here to shut the place down, are you?"

"I don't know. Any reason I should?"

Jack shrugged. "I'm sure you could find one if you looked hard enough. Wouldn't be no skin off my back, honestly. I've been feeling a career change lately."

"You been saying that for as long as I been coming here, Jack," said the flannel-wearing old man.

Jack gave the man a dismissive wave. "Can I get you anything? A soda or some water? Or I think I got some NAs in the back of the cooler, if you're partial to 'em."

Manuel wasn't. Non-alcoholic beers belonged in the same garbage bin as decaf coffee as far as he was concerned. He wasn't very partial to the fact his former struggles with alcoholism were such common knowledge in the area either, but his opponents never failed to bring it up each election cycle.

"I'm fine, thanks," he said. "But there is something I'd like to talk to you about."

"Should we go somewhere more private?" Jack asked.

"Right here's alright." At four o'clock on Thursday, The Sapphire Lounge was mostly empty, and Manuel didn't mind the few regulars around the bar who were most certainly eavesdropping. Maybe they'd seen something themselves.

"So, what's going on?" Jack asked. It was easy to tell he'd become a little nervous. The man had seen the back of a cop car a few times in his younger years, if memory served, and Manuel was pretty sure at least some of the ink on his arms was jailhouse art.

"Were you working that Friday night the Bobcats played Ashville? Would've been the night of November 17th."

"Unfortunately. Did get to listen to the game on the radio, though."

"You remember seeing these boys?" Manuel slid his phone across the bar.

Jack picked up the phone and took his time scrolling through the photos on the screen. "Yeah, I believe so. They look familiar."

"Do you remember if they left with anyone?"

Jack thought for a few seconds, then hummed and shook his head. "Mmmm, I honestly can't tell you, Sheriff. I worked a double that day, so I was dead on my feet at that point. Close to seeing pink elephants, you know? I don't think I even noticed 'em leaving."

"You talking 'bout them three young bucks from outta town?" Old Man Flannel asked.

Manuel swiveled a little in his stool to face him. "Did you see them?"

"Let me get a look at them pictures, and I can tell you certain." Manuel handed him the phone. He took it in his leathery hands and held it close to his face, peering over the top of his full-rim spectacles and squinting his eyes. "Yeah, I seen 'em, sure enough."

"Were they with anyone else?"

"Not most of the time, they weren't. Some woman came and sat down with 'em for a little while. I don't know if they left together or not, but they did leave 'bout the same time."

"What did she look like?" Manuel asked.

"She was a white woman. Brown hair, kind of short. Awful pretty."

"Are you talking about Charlotte Mallory?" Jack asked.

The name pricked Manuel's ears. He'd had two separate encounters with the woman since becoming Sheriff—both of them under the most suspicious of circumstances.

"Who?" the old man asked.

"Charlotte Mallory. You know, big-shot romance writer that owns that ranch near the old sawmill."

"Now, do I look like a man that reads romance novels?"

"You don't look like a man that reads at all, Gary. But just about everybody 'round here knows who Charlotte Mallory is."

"Ain't never heard of her," the old man...Gary, apparently... grumbled and went back to sipping his beer.

"Was Charlotte here that night, Jack?" Manuel asked.

"Believe so."

Manuel pulled out his phone again. All it took was googling the woman's name to pull up a hundred pictures of her from outlets like *The Guardian* and *Publishers Weekly*. "This who you saw them with?" Manuel asked, showing Gary the screen.

"Yeah, that's her. Daggum, pretty *and* rich? Sure do wish I had few less miles on the odometer."

"Gary, you couldn't have bagged that woman on the best day of your life," Jack said.

Gary stuck out his pale, bumpy tongue, like a geriatric child.

"You said you saw her leave with those boys?" Manuel asked.

"Nosir," Gary said. "I said they left around the same time. I didn't see where they went once they was out the door."

"Charlotte left her car here that night, though," Jack added. The exclamation in his tone suggested this detail had just come back to him. "She came by the next day and picked it up. Must have got an Uber home or something."

"Or something," Manuel said. "Hey, this place doesn't happen to have cameras, does it?"

Jack frowned and shook his head. "Owner's a cheap old bastard. Surprised he don't make me water down the whiskey."

"Bullshit you don't water the whiskey," said Gary.

"Thank you, gentlemen," Manuel said, standing up from the stool. "I appreciate the help." He left a few ones on the bar even though he hadn't ordered a drink, then he walked back out into the sunshine.

Staying there at that stool until they kicked him out—drinking the place dry—was what temptation told him to do. He took one last look at the welcoming lighted sign, then sighed and started his car. Instead, he was going to the last place on earth he wanted to visit, today or any day: Charlotte Mallory's cursed ranch.

57

9

Charlotte took a bite of her toast and thanked her sister for it, even though it tasted a little burnt. She'd been present one time to hear Lilibeth's husband tell her it wouldn't surprise him if she burned a fruit salad. She'd been there to see him take a hell of a tongue lashing for it too, and the last thing Charlotte needed this morning was to evoke Lilibeth's ire.

"It's the pits it's supposed to rain all day," Lilibeth said. She took a bite of her own well-blackened toast and swallowed it down as though it tasted just fine. "I was really hoping we could take the boys to the park and let them burn some energy off."

Out the picture window across from the table where they sat, the gray sky had been spitting a steady sprinkle of rain all morning. But if the raucous sounds from the living room were any indication, Malachi and his cousin Ethan were burning plenty of energy anyway.

"Next weekend's supposed to be nice at least," Charlotte said.

"Yeah, but JD's getting home next weekend."

"Oh right. I forgot." JD—Lilibeth's husband—worked a 21/21 schedule on an oil rig about ninety miles west of Hooper Valley, and Lilibeth never made plans on his first weekend home.

"I'm just glad they're able to play together again. I wasn't sure…" Lilibeth trailed off, then took another bite of her toast.

What she wasn't sure about, Charlotte knew, was how long after Deborah Vickers's death it would take before she was comfortable letting Ethan play with Malachi again. Two months turned out to be the answer. In the few times Charlotte had tried to arrange something before this weekend, Lilibeth always had some excuse ready.

Charlotte didn't blame her, really. That's why she'd kept trying instead of getting angry or giving up. It killed her to know that Malachi had witnessed something so horrific at such a young, formative age. It killed her even more not knowing exactly what he'd seen. If Lilibeth didn't want her son hanging out with him until enough time had passed to gauge the damage done, Charlotte completely understood.

If there'd been any damage at all, though, Malachi sure didn't show it. She'd watched him closely these past two months, every minute of the day. She'd taken him to a pediatric psychologist too, and her assessment had been the same: Malachi was too young to comprehend whatever he'd witnessed that night and would almost certainly not remember it as he grew older.

Truthfully, the thing that still bothered Charlotte the most was what he'd said to that old Hispanic sheriff. Malachi had told him that he did it. If that had been the only time, Charlotte surely could have written it off as childish garble or him not understanding the question. But there'd been one other time after that. Six days later when she was feeding Malachi his lunch, he'd told her that he had "poked Mish Deba in the belly" and that she "fell down."

"Children his age are highly egocentric," the psychologist had told her. "They see the world entirely through their own perspective. Just by virtue of being there, Malachi might feel responsible for Mrs. Vickers's death. That could explain the things he's said."

Charlotte couldn't decide whether that made sense to her or not. Whether she believed it. But whatever the explanation was, it was surely something along those lines: the ineffable workings of a toddler's mind.

"Anything new with the investigation?" Lilibeth asked, confirming her train of thought was on the same rail as Charlotte's. And confirming also what Charlotte knew she'd been about to say.

"Nothing. Not anything they've shared with me, anyway."

"It's just so awful. I mean, who would do that to a poor old woman?"

"I'd really rather not talk about it, Lils," Charlotte said. Lilibeth sniffed and took a sip of her coffee. Once more, Charlotte couldn't blame her. How could they talk about TV shows and town happenings with such an albatross in the air? Deborah Vickers's murder, after all, was the only happening anyone in town wanted to talk about.

"You really should speak to someone about it, though," Lilibeth said. "I know you've been so focused on making sure Malachi's alright, and that's completely understandable. But I'm sure it was traumatic for you too, Charlotte."

"Maybe you're right." She was certainly right about one thing: Charlotte had been focused solely on her son these past two months. To the point she'd not even begun to process what walking into the house that night and seeing what she'd seen had done to her own psyche.

"I don't know if it'd be weird or not," Lilibeth said, "both of us seeing the same therapist. But mine is this Native woman named Enola, and I love her. Full-blood Choctaw, can you believe it? I could give you her email if you want it."

"Sure," Charlotte said. She didn't know if she wanted to see this Enola woman, or any therapist for that matter, but, for now, it was easier to just agree.

"Hold on, I've got it saved in my phone." Lilibeth stood up from the kitchen table and started looking around the counters until she spotted her Kate Spade purse. Charlotte watched her unzip it and reach her hand inside.

That exact moment was when the screaming started—so shrill and anguished it sent a stream of terror like liquid nitrogen surging through Charlotte's heart. She saw Lilibeth drop both purse and phone as though they were the most inconsequential items in the world. Time seemed to turn glacial for that instant, the items falling frame by frame like a slow-mo shot in a movie.

Then the rush of air and rapid footsteps of Lilibeth racing past her broke Charlotte's momentary trance. The adrenaline dump hit her like a jolt of electricity, and Charlotte leapt from the chair. A hundred different nightmares of what might have happened to her child flew through her thoughts in rapid fire.

Yet Charlotte knew even before they made it to the living room that none of them were true. Malachi was not the one who'd been hurt. The screams were not his.

Rounding the corner, she saw Ethan lying on the living room floor, his mouth stretched open in a hitching scream and his face as red as a cherry. He was holding one hand in the other. An instant later, Charlotte realized why. One of the digits on his left hand was missing. His ring finger, it looked like. In the place where it should have been was empty space and a ragged stump still spurting blood like a water gun. Charlotte saw a flash of white bone and felt like she might faint.

"Ethan!" Lilibeth screamed. "Oh my god!" Ethan saw her and screamed even harder.

So much screaming, Charlotte thought, somewhere amidst all the chaos in her head. Was Malachi screaming too? She scanned the room for him and spotted him sitting on Lilibeth's rocker recliner.

"Charlotte!" In the corner of her eye, Charlotte could see her sister pulling Ethan's shirt off and wrapping it around his blood-soaked hand. "Help me!"

But Charlotte only half heard her. She couldn't take her eyes away from Malachi. Couldn't believe what they'd just seen. He stared back at her while he chewed. Even over all the screaming, she could hear the crunch of crushing bone.

"Charlotte! For God's sake, call an ambulance!"

This finally broke her trance. But not before she witnessed one last bewildering horror: her son's throat moving as he swallowed the masticated digit in a single, glugging gulp.

10

The sound of a knock at the front door made Charlotte's heart drop in her chest. She wasn't expecting company. Not now, not ever. Sometimes delivery drivers would knock or ring the bell, but she wasn't expecting any packages either.

There was another knock, a little harder. Then a voice behind it that chilled her even more.

"Wayne County Sheriff's Department. Can you come to the door, ma'am?"

Charlotte recognized that voice. Recognized the subtle Spanish accent of a man who'd grown up speaking English but still had it in his blood. Charlotte took a quick glance at the basement door to make sure it was closed, then another at the stairs. Malachi was up there in his bedroom, and she prayed that's where he'd stay. With the razor-honed senses she'd seen him demonstrate on plenty of occasions, he had certainly heard the knock. Now, she could only hope he would follow the rules.

It felt like she was sweating profusely, and she wiped her face with the hem of her sweater before she approached the front door. Through the frosted glass panel, she saw a tall figure wearing a cowboy hat. Her heart took that as a signal to gallop even faster.

Breathe, she told herself. Then she took a long inhale and opened the door.

"Ms. Mallory. I don't know if you remember me or not, but—"

"I remember you, Sheriff," Charlotte said, her voice perfectly calm and pleasant. That was good. A good start at least.

"You mind if I come in?"

Charlotte bit her bottom lip. "This is embarrassing, but the place is an absolute wreck. I've been so busy writing lately…"

Very funny, Charlotte's subconscious interjected; she hadn't written anything more than a grocery list in the better part of two years.

"…and now I'm so far behind on chores, it looks like a tornado came through. I think I'd drop dead from shame if you saw it."

She'd hoped the sheriff would chuckle or at least smile a little at this, but he didn't. "I can promise you I've seen worse, ma'am."

"Why don't we talk on the porch?" Charlotte said, stepping out the door and letting it close behind her. "It's nice enough out today."

Cold as a polar bear's toenails is what it was. She saw the way Sheriff Garcia cocked an eyebrow at her, and she cringed inwardly at how suspicious she must look. It was better than letting him inside, though. A search warrant was the only way that was happening.

"What can I do for you, Sheriff?" she asked, fighting back the shivers in her limbs. A gust of ice-laced wind stung her face and lifted her auburn hair from her shoulder.

"Do you remember going to The Sapphire Lounge a couple weeks ago? Would've been the night of November 17th."

Charlotte kept a straight face, but it felt like he'd just punched her in the gut. She'd hoped this visit had something to do with the Vickers investigation. Or a parking ticket, or a profession of love, or anything but what happened on November 17th.

"I don't recall the exact date, but I was there a couple weeks ago." Lying wouldn't have been the right move. If he was here and asking, then he already knew she'd been there. "Was that a Friday?"

"Yes, ma'am. There was a big football game going on in town that night."

"Oh, yeah. I remember now. And yes, I was there that night."

"Do you remember seeing these three boys there?" Sheriff Garcia asked, handing her his phone.

Charlotte had no need to look at the pictures—already knew whose faces she would see—but she scrolled through them anyway. "Yeah, I remember seeing them."

"Jack Godfrey says he seems to recall you having a few drinks with them."

Not good. But at least she'd learned this before she made the mistake of denying it. "Maybe. It's honestly hard to say, Sheriff. I had a few too many that night, I think. I ended up having to get my sister to come pick me up."

Nice opportunity to go ahead and establish that alibi, Charlotte figured.

"Did you see what time the boys left? Or if they were with anyone when they did?"

Charlotte feigned a moment's consideration. "Mmmm…I'm sorry, Sheriff. It's been so long ago. And, like I said, the whole night's a bit foggy."

"If you could remember anything at all worth mentioning, it'd be a big help."

"Why? Are those boys in some kind of trouble or something?"

"They've been reported missing. You and anyone else at The Sapphire Lounge that night are the last people known to have seen them."

"Really?" Charlotte said, satisfied she'd got the tone right; surprise had always been one of the hardest things for her to fake. "That's awful."

"Did you happen to see them talking to anyone else?"

"I mean, I'm sure they did. I wasn't really paying attention, to be honest."

"You said your sister picked you up, right? Remind me what her name is again."

"Lilibeth Wyatt. And yes, she gave me a ride home."

"You remember about what time that was?" the sheriff asked.

"Not exactly. Sometime around eleven."

"And the boys, did they leave about the same time?"

"Maybe. I really don't know. I'm sorry I can't be more help. I just…don't know anything helpful, I'm afraid."

The sheriff sighed. "Well, if you think of anything else…" He paused and chuckled just a little. For some reason, Charlotte didn't like the sound of it. "Well, you know the drill by now, don't you, Ms. Mallory?"

"I'm not sure I follow."

"I'm just saying, what with the Vickers murder and then your missing boy, this isn't our first rodeo together."

"I've experienced a lot of misfortune, Sheriff."

He watched her for a moment, his sharp eyes betraying a keen intelligence beneath all the wrinkles and backcountry demeanor. Then he sighed again and broke his gaze. "Yeah, I suppose you have. You were an orphan, right? I seem to remember reading that in an article somewhere."

"Yes. My parents were heroin addicts. CPS took Lilibeth and me when we were toddlers. They both overdosed before I turned seven."

"I'm sorry to hear that. One of the worst diseases there is. Addiction, I mean."

"I still resent them for it," Charlotte said. She wasn't sure why she was telling him all this. It'd just been so long since she'd talked with anyone about her parents that the words were tumbling out now. "They chose the drugs over their children. There's nothing I would choose over my child." Then, realizing that Malachi was gone as far as the sheriff was concerned, she added, "Nothing I wouldn't give to have him back."

The sheriff frowned and nodded knowingly. "I appreciate you taking the time to talk with me. You let me know if you remember anything else."

Charlotte watched him turn and start down the porch steps. She let out a silent exhale. Then cut it short when he turned around again.

"You know, I wasn't gonna bring this up, but you'll probably see it all over the papers soon anyhow. One of those missing boys is my little sister's kid. I haven't always been there for either one of them, and…" He stopped and sighed. Charlotte watched the cold turn the breath into white fog. Her own breath stayed sealed in her lungs, which were struck paralyzed for a moment along with the rest of her body. "Anyway. I just really want to find him."

Charlotte just stood there, a blank look on her face. She supposed she should say something, but even if the words had come, her tone would've surely given her away.

Sheriff Garcia got back in his car and drove away. Charlotte watched until he turned onto the highway, then she hurried back inside and closed and locked the door.

11

Every lawman learns to trust his instincts. But the problem is that instincts don't get warrants signed. Driving away from Charlotte Mallory's ranch, Manuel knew in his bones she was hiding something. He'd seen it in her eyes—that flare of fear and guilt that only the most experienced (or depraved) outlaws could truly hide.

For now, though, there was nothing more he could do. He decided he'd give her time to stew for a couple days, then see if he could get her to come in for further questioning. Beyond that, his hands were the only ones in cuffs.

It was most likely nothing anyway. If he had to guess, he'd say the woman was probably just embarrassed to admit she spent the night drinking with three boys half her age. Or maybe nervous that if she did, she'd get caught up in something messy. Aside from guilt, that was the most common reason people kept things from the cops: they just didn't want to get involved.

Still, something about that woman and her ranch gave him a bad feeling. It wasn't just a figure of speech; Manuel truly did believe the place was cursed.

First there'd been the Vickers woman, whose killer had still not been found. Then the boy's disappearance. Half the town had combed the area around her ranch for weeks looking for him and never found a trace. Now, the same woman at the epicenter of those events—both of them strong contenders for the strangest case he'd ever worked—was quite possibly the last person to have seen his nephew. For a man who didn't like coincidences, that wasn't easy to let go.

Maybe he'd track down her sister too. See what she had to say about that night. Later, though. Right now, all he could think about was his living room sofa and the bottle of Aleve on his nightstand. He could feel the first trace of a migraine coming on. It always started at the base of his neck and moved up from there. He probably needed to see a doctor about them. Sheer stubbornness was the only reason not to.

By the time he pulled into his apartment complex, the pain in his skull was hammering. It felt like someone was stabbing a pair of ice picks into his temples over and over. He staggered up the stairs to his second-story unit, then collapsed on the gray cloth couch as soon as he was inside.

He closed his eyes and put a hand over them, not only to block out the searing light from the window but to block his view of the place as well. His apartment was an absolute disaster. When he'd told Charlotte he was sure he'd seen places messier than hers, what he hadn't told her was that he'd meant his own.

Cups and plates lined the coffee table in front of the sofa, and there was garbage on the floor. If he ran his finger along any piece of furniture in the place, it would turn up an ungodly layer of dust. These living conditions might not have been the cause of his headaches, but they couldn't help. Your environment impacts your health. Or at least that's what he'd read on the computer.

He didn't know how he'd let it get this bad. Sure, it had taken some adjusting after the divorce. He and Violet had always split up the chores by designating some as his full-time responsibility and some as hers. But when she left him, he'd found himself responsible for things like dishes and vacuuming again for the first time in years.

It wasn't until lately, though, that he'd really started to let go of the rope. Keeping up with it all on top of a job that required more than full-time hours most weeks seemed to get harder every day. At sixty-seven years old, his body could hardly handle the strain.

Retirement called to him like death calls to the dying. But he couldn't go gently into that good night just yet. Not with the threads of something so big he could sense it still yet to be unraveled. If it was the last thing he did while wearing the badge, Sheriff Garcia was going to get to the bottom of it.

Right after he got rid of this damned headache, that is. And the best thing for that, he'd found, was a nice long nap. With so much to do, it was a shameful waste of time, but Manuel couldn't imagine doing anything else today until he'd rested his eyes a bit.

Sleep came quickly for him, but with it came dreams that made him toss and turn on the sofa the entire time. A trio of vivid nightmares all set on Charlotte Mallory's cursed ranch and all featuring the same subject: a monster with crocodile teeth and demon eyes. When Manuel woke sometime later slicked with sweat, the image stuck with him the rest of the day.

73

12

BEFORE

She was losing her mind. That was it, Charlotte decided. The relief she felt at deciding something that would've horrified most people almost made her laugh.

They'd probably come and lock her away in a padded room before long. Or was that something that only happened in the movies? She hoped not. The idea of it actually sounded kind of nice: being taken away and stripped of responsibility, cared for by others without a worry in the world.

But then what would become of Malachi? The thought of her son sent Charlotte crashing back down to reality. He was real, after all. Not a delusion or a figment of her imagination. What he did was real.

He had turned three last week. On his second birthday, Charlotte had weighed and measured him, but she'd been too afraid to do it this time. Afraid of how shocking the results were sure to be.

The boy stood well over head and shoulders above every child his age. Charlotte had recently taken to keeping him hidden away as best she could to avoid drawing attention. Soon she would need a more permanent solution.

It wasn't just his size, though, that caused her to question her sanity. Charlotte could have accepted that. That could've been explained by some genetic disorder. Maybe even treated. But the rest had no rational explanation. The feats of impossible speed and strength she'd seen her son display at such a young age. The darkness she'd seen within him.

The...*appetites* he'd demonstrated.

They're gonna lock you away, Charlie, sang the voice in her head. *You're craaaazy*.

She watched out the kitchen window as Malachi played with his trucks in the backyard sandbox. He looked so ordinary, save for his size. Like a perfectly normal child. And most days, that's exactly what he was. But there were other times. Times when something else seemed to overtake him. A darkness and a hunger that terrified her to her core.

It had overtaken him again just last week. He had screamed and slammed his fists and begged for food yet had furiously rejected everything she offered. Bowls of Goldfish were sent flying into the air; spoons of applesauce slapped away. On and on it went like this for hours. And all the while, Charlotte had sensed somewhere deep down exactly what her son wanted.

She'd felt like a madwoman walking him out to the stables. Like the entire trek through the sputtering rain with thunder rumbling in the distance and darkness falling over the fields was some kind of hallucination she'd snap out of any instant.

The horses had all acted jittery when she and Malachi walked into the stable. Like they could sense the same thing she could. Charlotte had always had a lot of respect for horses, for their awareness and intelligence. It made doing what she'd done almost as painful as the alternative she'd been preventing.

She'd watched as Malachi approached the nearest stall and set his hand on the thick, muscular neck of the horse poking out its head. A chestnut mare named Lucy that Charlotte had raised from a foal. She'd been stamping and whinnying as he approached, but the moment Malachi touched her flesh, she never moved a muscle. He had whispered something into her perked ear. Charlotte had not been able to hear the words, but she watched as Lucy's large, almost human eyes turned crazed.

What happened next happened so fast it boggled the mind: a terrible cracking sound like a dry branch snapping and a wet ripping sound like…like a horse's entire head being torn off its body. There was nothing else in the world to compare that sound to. When she closed her eyes at night, she could still hear it.

And the blood. She couldn't believe how much there had been. It had sprayed out from Lucy's severed neck like a firehose, showering Malachi and the stable walls from top to bottom as her body jerked and her back legs kicked sporadically.

Then Malachi had leapt over the stall's gate and out of Charlotte's sight. She had only heard what came next, not daring to walk up and see it with her eyes. The sounds of tearing and chewing and swallowing left little to the imagination anyway.

It wasn't until that moment that her mind accepted what her heart had already known to be true: that her son was something more than a little baby boy. Something frightening and inexplicable, defying all reason.

She supposed she shouldn't be so shocked. His very birth after the doctors had told her at a young age she'd never conceive defied all reason too.

And so did the boy's father.

Thinking of him sent a chill down the back of Charlotte's neck and caused her to physically shudder. It killed her that she could see him in Malachi—his features, his skin, his hair. It became most evident those times when the darkness overtook him. It was haunting to see those same flames she'd seen before in the eyes of her own son.

For now, though, he was just a boy playing in a sandbox. Charlotte wondered how long it would last this time before his hunger returned and feared it would not be long; he'd told her himself that his previous meal was "just okay." She knew without him having to say it what the darkness within him truly hungered for.

And if she didn't provide it, there was no way to stop him from going out and taking it himself.

That was her ultimate justification for the decision she'd already made. She could keep him hidden away. Keep him safe from the world and keep the world safe from him. But only if she provided for all his needs.

Only if she hunted for him.

She would choose her targets carefully. Not only those that presented the least amount of risk, but also those that deserved it. Criminals and cheaters and abusers. How she'd pull that off—how she'd pull any of it off—Charlotte had not the faintest clue. One step at a time, though, right? That's the only way to go when you're going through hell.

Malachi caught eyes with her through the window then and gave her a snaggle-tooth smile. She smiled back, but fear shot through her veins in icy spurts. She had seen those teeth elongate and sharpen like those of a vampire or werewolf in a movie. Except this wasn't a movie, and the blood he'd spilled with those predator teeth was warm and real.

Charlotte turned off the kitchen sink and set her drying rag down on the counter, deciding it was time for Malachi to come in. She'd have to keep a close watch on him from now on. If she let him out of her sight—if she allowed him to wander away down the highway and into town—there was no telling what would happen.

"Malachi," she said, leaning out the back door. "It's time to come inside."

"Fives more minutes!" Malachi shouted while he worked on digging a hole in the sand big enough to bury his Tonka dump truck.

"No, I want you to come inside now, baby." Malachi puffed out his lip and glared at her. For an instant—if her own eyes weren't playing tricks on her—she saw those black flames in his eyes again. "Right now, Malachi. You do what I tell you."

To her relief, he listened. As he brushed the sand from his shorts and trudged begrudgingly across the yard, Charlotte thought of what she would do when the day came that he didn't listen. He was already stronger than her. Stronger than ten of her. If she was going to keep him in check, her methods would have to be mental rather than physical. Like how circuses used to keep ele-phants tied up with flimsy little ropes. And the elephants, who could've snapped them like dental floss, never did. Because they never realized they could.

That would take a lot of time and careful planning. And, for right now, there were more pressing problems to fix. As she watched all five foot of her three-year-old son stomp across the yard like a juvenile giant, she knew the day was coming soon when she could let no one else see him.

Fortunately, Charlotte had a plan for that too.

13

BEFORE

Sheriff Garcia sat at Charlotte Mallory's dining room table and studied her out of the corner of his eye. She looked like a wreck: hair disheveled, eyes red, tear stains on her cheeks. Everything you'd expect from a mother whose child was missing. Funny then, that something about her still didn't sit quite right with him.

"And what time did you wake up from your nap, Ms. Mallory?" he asked, looking up from his notepad.

"Ten minutes after three. I remember looking at the clock."

"And your son was already gone?"

"Yes," she said. "He was asleep in his bed when I laid down. That was the first place I looked. Then I checked the rest of the house and the yard, then the barn and stables. That's when I called the police."

"I know we haven't found anything out there yet, but him wandering off into the woods is still the most likely explanation," Manuel said.

But that grew less and less true with every minute that passed, if it was even still true at all. There must have been a hundred men and women—cops, firefighters, and plenty of volunteers from town—combing the woods surrounding the Mallory ranch for the past four hours. Even with a good head start, a three-year-old couldn't have made it far, and odds were they would have found him by now if he was out there.

"Do you remember hearing anything while you were lying down? Doors opening, vehicles pulling up...anything at all."

Charlotte shook her head. "I was exhausted, Sheriff. I was out like a light as soon as my head hit the pillow."

"I want you to think really hard about this, okay?" Manuel said. "And be really honest, too. Is there anyone you know of who would have a reason to take him?"

Charlotte shook her head again, but slower this time. "There's no one. His father, maybe, but...you already know that story."

Manuel did. He'd been keen to get in touch with the boy's father after the Deborah Vickers killing, but Charlotte had been able to tell him next to nothing about the man. She didn't even know his name.

"I need you to try and give me something about this man, Ms. Mallory," he said. "A name, a photograph, a place of previous employment. Right now, he's suspect number one."

And you're suspect number two, Manuel thought. He wouldn't say that part out loud, but he got the sense that Charlotte knew it anyway.

"He drove a Lincoln Continental," Charlotte said. "An older one, but it still looked brand-new. And it was black."

"I don't guess you remember the plate number." But the look in her eyes told him the answer before he'd even got the words out. "Well," Manuel sighed. "It's a start."

In reality, it was next to nothing. Without a name or any other way to identify the man, finding some drifter who'd wandered through Hooper Valley three years and nine months ago was virtually impossible.

"Do you think this has anything to do with whoever killed Mrs. Vickers?" Charlotte asked. Her voice shook a little, her fear clear to see. "Do you think they came back?"

"I can't say for certain," Manuel said. "But whoever killed Deborah Vickers, they left your son alone when they could have easily taken him or done something to him then. It would be awful strange for them to come back for him now."

But stranger things had happened. They happened all the time in the world of psychopaths and criminals. The fact the Vickers murder had gone unsolved this long still gnawed at Manuel all the time. The complete lack of evidence—no reliable witnesses, no DNA, no sign of forced entry or unidentified tire tracks on the road—bothered him even more; murders went unsolved all the time, but murders committed by phantoms were a lot rarer air.

"There is one place we haven't looked yet," Manuel said. "Inside the house."

Did he notice something then in Charlotte's expression? Maybe her eyebrows lifting just a little in worry or surprise?

"I've looked everywhere in here already, Sheriff," she said. "If he was in the house, I would've found him by now."

"What about the basement?" Manuel had passed by the door to it on his way through the house, and it had given him an odd feeling. Not the door itself or the fact the house had a basement—nothing out of the ordinary there—but the thick padlock bolting it closed was certainly a little odd.

"No," Charlotte said. "He couldn't have gotten down there. There are some guns down there, some cleaning chemicals, rat poison, things like that I don't want Malachi getting into. So, I keep the basement door locked."

"He could have found the key."

Charlotte shook her head. "The door's still locked, Sheriff. I checked it. There's no way he could have locked it back from the inside."

Unless he wasn't the one who locked it, Manuel thought. Between the way the lock on that door had caught his eye and the subtle way Charlotte's behavior had changed when he mentioned it, it made him curious.

"Mind if I take a look down there myself?"

Charlotte hesitated. Just for an instant, but Manuel still noticed. "Yeah, if you want to. I'll just have to go get the key."

"Alright," Manuel said.

Again, another heartbeat's hesitation. But then Charlotte stood and walked out of the kitchen. Manuel watched her until she turned the corner, then listened to her footsteps going up the stairs.

If she was willing to show him the basement, then chances were there was nothing down there. Then again, people consented to searches all the time knowing full well they were carrying dope or guns or something else that was going to get them locked up. Whether they didn't understand their rights or just didn't want to look suspicious, he'd seen it a hundred times before.

Manuel waited. Whatever she was doing up there, she was taking a long time. He pulled out his phone and thumbed through the notifications, but there weren't any worth clicking on.

From the light through the kitchen window, it seemed the sun had fully set. It was dim and reddish orange, and shadows were starting to fill the space. He thought about that three-year-old kid alone out there in the woods. If that's where he was, he'd probably have to spend the night out there; finding him in the dark would take a stroke of unlikely luck.

A couple of minutes later, he heard Charlotte coming back down the stairs. Manuel stood up. In the silence of the kitchen, the sound of his joints groaning and cracking was a stark reminder of how old he was getting.

Then, another sound perked his ears: the front door swinging open.

"Sheriff? You in here?" The voice belonged to Deputy Rickard. And the eagerness in it set Manuel's heart beating a little faster.

"Yeah. In the kitchen."

There were quick footsteps across the room, then Deputy Rickard rounded the corner. He looked winded, which was no surprise given the extra hundred pounds or so of excess weight he carried. How he passed his annual physical, Manuel had no idea. But right now, all he cared about was whatever the man seemed dying to blurt out. As soon as he caught his breath.

"We found something." Another deep breath. "In the woods. Been trying to radio you but—"

"I left it in the car," Manuel said. "What'd you find?"

"Kid's beanie hat. One of the volunteers found it in some bushes 'bout forty, fifty foot into the woods behind the stables."

Just then, Charlotte came into the kitchen. "Did you find him?" she asked, her eyes full of hope.

"No, ma'am," Deputy Rickard said, looking regretful. "Just a hat."

"What did it look like?" Manuel asked.

"Yellow with blue stripes."

Manuel looked at Charlotte. "Did he have one like that?"

"Maybe," she said. "I'd have to see it."

"Alright," Manuel said. "Let's go take a look then."

On the way out, he passed by the basement door again. He noticed it again, too, with its lock so polished and shiny it had to have been recently installed. He almost stopped, almost asked Charlotte if she'd found that key, but then she and Deputy Rickard were already out the front door. Casting one last glance at the padlock on his way past, Manuel followed them out.

14

BEFORE

It was three a.m. before Charlotte felt safe opening the basement door. The hours had passed as slowly as she imagined they would for someone being tortured to death. For twelve of them, an entire half day, she had kept her baby locked up alone in a dark basement, unable to hear his cries. Refusing to answer them when she began to hear them anyway in her soul.

Finally, the search party had gone home for the night. As soon as the last vehicle left her property, Charlotte rushed for the basement door like a sprinter at the gun.

She swiped the keys out of her pocket and hurried to open the lock, thinking all the while how fortunate she was that it was her opening it and not the sheriff. When he asked to see the basement, her plan had been to pretend she couldn't find the key. Who knows if it would have worked, and it wouldn't have been a good look either way. But then a stroke of blind luck had saved the day.

Someone had found the hat Malachi lost last month, and it had captured everyone's attention. Including the attention of Sheriff Garcia.

With the basement door unlocked, Charlotte threw it open and turned on the light. Immediately, the sight at the bottom of the stairs brought her to tears. Locking Malachi in an old dog crate, covering it with the extra soundproof panels, had broken her heart. Seeing it now, knowing how long she'd left him there, was even more heartrending.

Sobbing, almost tripping and tumbling the last few steps instead of walking them, Charlotte hurried down the stairs. She tore away the panel she'd taped to the crate's front side and looked into the dark enclosure, desperate to see Malachi alive and well.

He was sitting up—that's all she could tell for now—but it was enough to bring a wave of relief. Charlotte fumbled with the crate's latch and flung open its door. She crawled over the blanket she'd spread across its wire floor on all fours, then dove on Malachi, pulling him into her arms.

"I'm so sorry! I'm so sorry, baby!" Charlotte buried her face in his soft hair and sobbed into it.

She could smell the mess in his diaper. No telling how long he'd been sitting in his own filth. And though she'd left him a sippy cup full of milk, it looked like he hadn't touched it.

"Come on, Malachi. Let's go." Charlotte helped him out of the crate, then lifted him up into her arms. She struggled at first, and her heart dropped for an instant when it seemed he might drop as well; the days of her picking him up and carrying him were quickly coming to an end.

After bathing and changing him, feeding him a late-night dinner of all his favorite foods, and apologizing with every other breath, Charlotte tucked Malachi into bed and sat next to him on the bedside.

"Do you want Momma to read you a story?" Malachi just looked up at her sleepily. He'd barely spoken since coming out of the basement. He was tired, undoubtedly, and probably a little confused. But Charlotte couldn't help but interpret his silence as resentment.

She read him one anyway, if only to make herself feel better. A copy of *The Very Hungry Caterpillar* that she pulled from his small bookshelf by the bed. And though her voice was hoarse and strained with emotion, she still did her best to act out all the parts.

Malachi's eyes were closed by the end of the story, but she could tell he had not fully fallen asleep yet by the pattern of his breathing. She lay down beside him, snuggling in close.

"Momma?" he muttered while she stroked his arm.

"What is it?" she whispered back.

"I'm getting hungry again."

Charlotte just hugged him tighter and didn't say anything. Then, when Malachi's breathing finally settled into the rhythmic pattern of sleep, she quietly cried herself to sleep as well.

15

"I'm hungry again, Momma." Those dreaded words bounced around in Charlotte's mind like bullets ricocheting.

She'd known they were coming soon. Five months had passed since Malachi's last feeding. It was always unpredictable when his hunger would return, but two to three feedings per year was the average. And when it did come back—when he voiced his needs and gave her that regretful yet unyielding look—it always came back with a fury.

Eight days was the longest she had ever gone from the time Malachi made the request to the time she fulfilled it. That had happened last January. There'd been a point there towards the end where Charlotte genuinely feared that, if she didn't capture someone soon, he was going to eat her.

That or strike off on his own. Follow the road into town. Charlotte felt sick every time she thought of the possibility. The streets would flow with blood if she ever let it happen.

At seven years old now and officially six feet tall (she'd measured him just three days ago at the halfway mark to his eighth birthday), his strength was growing exponentially. She'd seen him bend a crowbar into a circle like it was a piece of wire. Seen him jump halfway up the trunks of full-grown trees and scamper the rest of the way to the top at a speed that would've made even the most agile tree-dwellers envious.

Seen him rip grown men limb from limb like rotisserie chickens.

He's getting stronger in other ways, too, Charlotte thought, ushering that last awful image from her mind. It was his mind she was thinking of now. Not just his perception and intelligence (though these were growing in leaps and bounds as well) but something more. Something she couldn't quite understand.

She had witnessed him use his mental abilities on others. And, to some extent, she'd *felt* him use them on her. It was always subtle, something as simple as bringing him an ice cream bar or turning cartoons on the TV when that's not really what she meant to do. Somehow—in some indescribable way—Malachi had a way of getting inside your head and making you do what he wanted. Faintly, like a whisper in her subconscious, she could almost hear him sometimes, speaking his will into her thoughts.

She could feel it now as she strode toward the basement door, a needle-tipped syringe in her hand. During times like this, it was almost as if his hunger became her hunger. His dark desires hers as well. It happened like this each time; Charlotte figured that was part of the reason why it had become so easy to do what she did.

The lights were already on in the basement. She always kept them on during the day and turned them off at night, trying to give her guests…

Prisoners, Charlie. Let's not be disingenuous.

…some semblance of a day-night cycle. She spotted them both right away. Not like the chains around their ankles let them go very far. But neither of them even looked up as she came down the stairs.

The boys were used to her coming and going by now. Used to her bringing them food and books and board games, putting movies on the basement television and cleaning out the camp toilet they used. Charlotte had been walking up and down these stairs so often lately, the muscles in her calves were starting to grow.

She did tuck the syringe behind her back as she came down, though; they wouldn't be used to seeing that.

When she made it to the last step, Zion finally looked up from the card game he and Clint were playing on the floor. It hit her then how badly what she was about to do would hurt him. How it would ultimately hurt him even more than Clint, who would suffer only moments before his pain ended while Zion was forced to carry on alone.

"What's up?" Zion asked, his voice mostly calm but with that fearful edge to it that no amount of her trips down here could take away.

Charlotte approached, stepping past the point in the basement where she knew their chains could reach if either of them were to jump up and charge her.

They knew better than to try something like that. She'd made sure they understood the reality of their situation. Made it clear that she never carried her phone or the keys to their shackles on her when she came down to the basement. If, somehow, they managed to get their hands on her—hurt her, kill her—all they'd be doing is dooming themselves to starvation.

What they'd really be dooming themselves to was Malachi's wrath. Which she supposed was their fate anyway. But they didn't know that.

"Your friend is being released today," Charlotte said to Zion. She watched Clint as she spoke, saw the combination of hope and distrust in his eyes.

She'd told them that's what happened to the other one, Luke Howler. That he had been released. Charlotte wasn't sure if they actually believed it, but she could tell they wanted to. That was enough to at least help keep them compliant.

"I'm not leaving unless he gets to leave too," Clint said. And despite the slight quiver in his voice, she could tell he mostly meant it.

"That's not my call," Charlotte said.

She'd been putting on this act of being part of some larger operation ever since she brought them down here, pretending she wasn't allowed to tell them much, hinting at some bigger scheme and letting their imaginations fill in the gaps. It made things easier that way.

"What's in your hand?" Zion asked.

Charlotte pursed her lips. He was an observant one; must run in the family. Then she brought her hand up from her side and showed him the syringe.

"The hell is that for?" Clint asked.

"I'm going to sedate you," Charlotte said. "You'll be placed in the back of a car and driven by two men to a rest center several hours from here. There will be a pay phone there you can use to call for help when you wake up."

"Fuck that," Clint said, shaking his head and glaring at her.

Charlotte took a step back toward the stairs. "Or you can stay down here for a few more months. I'm sure the organization wouldn't mind postponing your release." Clint swallowed and glanced at Zion, clearly unsure. "Your choice," she added.

"I'm staying," Clint said, looking suddenly resolute.

Charlotte frowned. "Alright…well, then it's not your choice. I lied. You're coming with me."

Clint's upper lip lifted a little, exposing his teeth. He had a wild glint in his eye that Charlotte didn't like one bit. "Make me, bitch."

Charlotte grinned. And though it shocked her that she did it, it felt good. Somewhere deep within her thoughts, she could feel Malachi there with her. Urging her on.

She bent over and set the syringe down on the floor. Then she gave it a hard push. It rolled across the concrete and came to a stop at Clint's shoe.

"Take it," she said, her tone and glare daring him to defy her. "Stick it your arm. Or you and your friend won't eat again for a week." She could hear him gritting his teeth, could see the muscles in his jaws quivering as he did. "Two weeks."

"Go to hell," Clint spat, never even glancing at the syringe. But then Zion reached over and picked it up for him. Charlotte watched, curious what he'd do. She thought he might try to convince his friend, maybe even stick it in him himself. Instead, he flipped her the bird with one hand and slowly depressed the syringe's plunger with the other until the last of the clear liquid streamed out the needle's end.

Charlotte didn't blink, but, on the inside, she was starting to panic. She'd been too smug, overplayed her hand, and now she was up shit creek. That was the only dose of Ketamine she had, and getting more from her sister would take days.

Before she could begin to think of how she planned to get a fully alert, fully noncooperative man twice her size and strength all the way out to the barn, Charlotte heard the basement door creak open. She saw Clint and Zion both look up, one squinting and the other raising his eyebrows.

She knew what they saw without having to turn around, but she looked over her shoulder anyway. Malachi stood at the top of the stairs. He stared down into the basement unblinking, but not at her. His eyes were locked on Clint.

"Come play with me," he said.

Clint's mouth came open like he was going to speak, then went slack. He stammered for a moment, then stopped and swallowed hard. Beads of sweat began to break out on his skin, and the color slowly faded from his face.

"Hey! Hey, what's going on?" Zion shouted, wide eyes fixed on his friend.

"Let's go," said Malachi.

Clint only nodded, his gaze somewhere distant now.

Malachi threw something at him then. Not hard—if he'd wanted to, Charlotte figured he could have thrown whatever it was hard enough to tear through Clint like a bullet—but just an underhand toss that landed the item in his lap. Charlotte recognized it when Clint picked it up; it was the key to his shackle, distinguishable from the one that unlocked Zion's by the little piece of red tape she'd put around it. She'd planned on going back up for it once Clint was sedated, but Malachi must have known where she hid it all along.

Without a word or any hesitation, Clint picked up the key and unlocked his shackle. It slid from his ankle and clattered to the floor. He stood, and Charlotte took a cautious step back. But there was no malice in his eyes. There was nothing there at all. They looked as empty as the eyes of someone spaced out on heavy drugs. Or the eyes of the dead. He walked past Charlotte without seeming to notice her, then started up the stairs.

"Clint!" Zion shouted. "What are you doing, bro? Run!"

But Clint kept the same leisurely pace. When he neared the top of the stairs, Malachi reached out his hand. Charlotte and Zion both watched equally amazed as Clint took it and let Malachi lead him away.

16

You get used to things, even when they're terrible. For the past five months (159 days if you were counting, and he certainly was), Zion had mostly got used to living in the nameless woman's basement.

The chains and never seeing the sunlight were a bitch. And the woman who'd brought them down here (she'd introduced herself as Laura, but Zion had noticed the way she reacted to that name enough times to know it wasn't her real one) was *definitely* a bitch—even if she did cook good food. In reality, all of it was pretty bad if you think about it. But that's the thing; eventually, Zion had stopped thinking about it.

He and Clint had watched movies and played video games (offline only, of course), read books, and ate their three not-bad-at-all meals a day without a single responsibility. Once the fear and anger had run their course, parts of it began to feel like being a kid again, in a kind of good way.

Now that Clint was gone, the mirage had started to dissolve. It was hitting him all at once, all those negative emotions he'd been pushing down, and he was having a hard time catching his breath.

He slumped against the basement wall. There was a sofa The Bitch had moved down here not far away, within reach of his chain, but he didn't feel he had the strength to get there. The walls he saw every minute of the day were closing in on him. The wood plank ceiling with its single, buzzing bulb at the center started to spin.

Luke was dead. Clint was going to die, if he wasn't dead already. And Zion would be dead too before he ever left this place. He and Clint had let themselves believe out of want The Bitch's bullshit about eventually setting them free, but they'd both known the truth deep down. She had shown them her face. They knew where she lived. That meant there was no chance she'd ever let them go.

It took several minutes for his panic attack to pass. He nearly threw up on the floor at one point and would have if for no other reason than to piss off The Bitch. But Zion hated throwing up. Hated it so much that the fear of it had probably saved him from a lot of excess drinking over the years.

Still taking deep breaths, he gazed up at the top of the basement stairs. What had he seen there? It had looked like a little kid. A *huge* little kid, though.

And it wasn't just his size or appearance that set Zion's hairs on end—it was the way it had felt towards the end when the kid, or whatever he was, told Clint to come with him. Something had overtaken his friend, and Zion had felt it too: a warm, buzzy sensation almost like being drunk. Drunk and highly impressionable. If the boy had asked *him* to come up those stairs, Zion probably would have done it too. He probably would've wrapped the chain around his neck and choked himself to death if he'd been told to. Knowing this was true made his head spin.

Maybe The Bitch wasn't lying. Maybe she really was part of some secret organization, and that kid was the result of some mad scientist experiment.

Or maybe he'd just read too many comics as a boy. None of it made any sense any way you looked at it, and Zion had the depressing feeling he'd probably die before he found out the answer.

But not before he took The Bitch out with him.

He and Clint had talked about it plenty of times. And there had been plenty of opportunities. She never even bothered to arm herself when she came down. Nevertheless, she had held a pretty frightening sword over their heads: starvation.

As far as he could tell, what she'd told them was true: she never brought her phone or keys down to the basement. Which meant that killing her wouldn't help them escape but would ensure they never saw another meal. Zion had suffered through a seventy-two-hour fast one time, and he could only imagine the horror that starving to death would slowly become. Even worse, he'd known what would inevitably happen—what always happened when two or more people were starving no matter how righteous or fond of one another they were.

But now Clint was gone, and Zion had seen things that frightened him even more than starving. He didn't have much in the way of a plan. But then again, he didn't really need one; next time The Bitch stepped within his reach, Zion was going to smash her head against the floor and let all the crazy spill out of it.

Still leaning against the wall, he let the thought of this soothe him. Whatever insanity was happening here, it would be over soon. Over for him, at least. And, if he had anything to say about it, over for her too.

17

"Ready or not, here I come!" Malachi shouted from the living room. Crouched behind the bed in her room, Charlotte realized that the top of her head was probably showing, but she didn't bother adjusting her position; Malachi always found her in seconds no matter how well she hid.

And truthfully, she wasn't much in the mood for games anyway. It had taken the entire morning to clean up the mess Malachi had left behind in the barn, hauling away the larger chunks in trash bags, shoveling up the stained sawdust, and wiping the walls with bleach.

The trouble was that Malachi always got playful after a feeding. As though the darkness that built in him as his hunger grew left all at once as soon as that hunger was satiated. Charlotte, who denied him any other source of companionship, could never tell him no.

"Found you!" Malachi shouted, leaping onto the bed and leaning over its edge. His face appearing suddenly right in front of hers made Charlotte jump.

"You sure did," she said once she caught her breath.

"Your turn!"

"How about we take a little break, okay? Then we'll play again after."

"Promise?"

"Promise," Charlotte said as she sat down on the bed beside him. "Momma's just getting old."

Malachi giggled. "Is your hair gonna turn white, Momma? Like Mural on Courage the Cowardly Dog?"

"*Murial,*" Charlotte corrected. "And I'm honestly surprised it hasn't turned white already, kiddo."

"Because of me, right?" Malachi asked, flopping back on the bed.

Charlotte stared at him, a little stunned but not all that surprised. She often forgot how perceptive he could be; slipping little inuendoes past him wasn't as easy as it was with most kids his age.

"No, baby." Charlotte wrapped an arm around him and smiled, doing her best to make the lie believable. "Not because of you."

Malachi studied her. He looked sad. And guilty. And Charlotte harbored no doubt that those piercing dark eyes of his could see the same feelings in her.

"Can I ask you something?" he said.

"Yeah," Charlotte said.

"Is it wrong to hurt people?"

Charlotte's mind swam through a sea of thoughts and possible responses. So many questions that children ask are difficult for parents to answer. In her situation, the questions Malachi asked (and would continue to ask as he grew older) were infinitely more challenging.

"Most of the time, it's wrong," Charlotte said. "But there are exceptions sometimes."

"What's a seption?" Malachi asked.

"*Exception*," Charlotte said. Then she lifted her eyes to the ceiling while she thought of a good way to explain. "You know how most days in the summertime are really hot, but then there's some days that are rainy and cold?" Malachi nodded. "That's an exception. It's like when something is usually true, but then sometimes it isn't."

Charlotte figured she probably butchered that explanation, but Malachi seemed to understand anyway.

"What about when I hurt people?" he asked. "Is that an exception?"

The way he looked at her, it was all she could do to keep her eyes from filling with tears. There was guilt and uncertainty scrawled all over his face. If the world saw her son, if it saw what he was and the things he did, he'd be regarded as a monster. No one but her would ever take the time to see him for who he was: a confused and frightened child who never asked to be born different.

"You remember that nature show we watched a few days ago?" Charlotte asked, taking a deep breath and discreetly wiping her eyes. "The one with the lions and the zebras?"

"Yeah."

"You remember when the lions went on a hunt? And they killed that one zebra because he was slower than the rest and they caught up to him."

Malachi nodded.

"Some animals like zebras eat grass, and some animals like lions need to kill other animals and eat their meat. And it isn't wrong, it's just…the way the world is. Does that make sense?"

"I guess, Momma."

Charlotte smoothed down a stray tuft of his dark, wavy hair. "You're special, Malachi. Special in ways I don't even understand myself. You're like one of those lions. And everyone else in the world are zebras. But here's the *super* important part, okay? Do you remember what happened when the lions caught the zebra?"

"They ate it," Malachi said in a "stating the obvious" tone.

"That's right. They didn't chase after the rest. They didn't kill any more than they had to. Just enough to fill their tummies. That's how you know if hurting someone is right or wrong. If you do it to survive, it's okay. If you do it for fun, it's wrong."

That was a far stretch from the lessons in morality Charlotte had been taught as a kid. A far stretch from what she'd ever imagined teaching her own child. But morals and survival didn't always coexist when met with violent reality. Sometimes surviving means killing a creature who wants to survive just as bad as you. Other times it means killing the version of yourself you used to be.

"What if it's both?" Malachi asked.

"What do you mean, baby?"

"I don't hurt people because it's fun, but…what if it's fun anyway?"

Charlotte hugged him tighter, even though his long, bony body felt suddenly cold in her arms. She changed the subject, asked if he'd like to resume their game of hide and seek, to which Malachi enthusiastically agreed.

Charlotte was supposed to count to twenty while he ran away and hid, but instead she just lay there on the bed for a while with her eyes closed. She remembered something her mother had said one time, back when Charlotte was a kid: that there weren't any handbooks on how to raise a child. Charlotte understood the sentiment even though she found it a little funny since there were literal handbooks galore on the topic of parenting. But when it came to raising a son like hers, there truly was no source of counsel. Not a single other soul in the world ever had to answer the questions she faced.

When she figured twenty seconds had passed (probably closer to a minute really), Charlotte got up and went to look for Malachi. Though not as quickly as he typically found her, she usually didn't have to look for him very long either; there were only so many places in the house a six-foot-tall boy could hide.

This time, she found him behind the curtains of the living room window. She'd spotted his feet sticking out from beneath them and had crept up to him even though she knew Malachi could sense her every step. When she swept the curtain aside and revealed him, he still squealed as though he was surprised.

They played until Malachi grew tired of the game, which, as always, took quite a long time. Charlotte didn't mind, though. It made him happy, and, for the brief moments she managed to push all other thoughts aside, it made her happy too.

She checked the time on her phone, saw it was nearly six, and realized she needed to get dinner started. Malachi could easily skip most meals. Though he did eat most days for the pleasure of it (and perhaps for other reasons Charlotte had not yet deciphered), she didn't think he actually got much sustenance from ordinary food. It was the other feedings that kept him nourished.

She was fine missing dinner every now and then too. But Zion needed to be fed. Yesterday—losing his friend—had been hard for him.

In the kitchen, she smushed a pound of hamburger meat into three patties while Malachi played with his toys at the table. She listened to him while she worked; his giggles and acted-out lines and whooshing explosion sounds as he smashed his action figures together were like music to distract her.

She didn't realize how hungry she was until the meat began to brown and its smell wafted through the kitchen. But she decided to feed Zion first instead of letting his get cold while she and Malachi ate.

At the basement door, Charlotte's heartbeat picked up. Things had reached a certain civility between her, Zion, and Clint. Now that Clint was gone, that civility would probably be gone too.

She set the plate and bottle of Dr. Pepper she was carrying down on the floor and opened the lock. The door creaked loudly as it opened, announcing her arrival. Charlotte made a mental note to give its hinges a squirt of WD-40 when she got the chance.

Gathering the food and drink again, she heard the scrape of chains against concrete from the bottom of the stairs. Charlotte marched down them, determined to keep a brave face even though she dreaded facing Zion after what had happened yesterday.

He was standing near the two mattresses on the floor she had brought down. The notion of removing the one Clint had slept on crossed Charlotte's mind. But, then again, there was no harm in just leaving it.

He watched her intently, but he didn't say anything. Charlotte locked eyes with him for a moment, then looked away. She walked up to the invisible line on the floor where she knew his chain could reach and set the plate and bottle down. She might have trusted him and his friend enough to cross that boundary before, but things had changed now. The truth of that was evident all over Zion's face.

"I hope you like it," Charlotte muttered, though she doubted she'd said it loud enough for him to hear from across the room. She turned back toward the stairs. But then Zion called out to her just as her back was turned. Plenty loud enough to hear.

"Hey!"

Charlotte almost kept going, but the kind of courtesy that comes impulsively to those who are naturally courteous made her stop. "What?" she asked.

"I want to know how you did it."

"Did what?"

"Killed my friends," Zion said. "I know you did, so don't bother lying. I just want to know how they died. I think I deserve to know that, right? Seeing as you're gonna kill me too."

Charlotte stared at him, her face frozen in an expression that didn't convey a single one of the thoughts and feelings swirling around in her head. With Zion's fierce yet so human, so *boyish*, eyes boring into her, she finally settled on something between the truth and lie.

"They died quickly," she said, then fast walked away back up the stairs.

18

Just before the first glint of dawn, Manuel grabbed his keys off the kitchen counter and headed out the door. He paused on the way out and glanced at the picture he'd thumbtacked just above the frame. It was a picture of Zion in his little league uniform the summer before he started high school. Manuel had printed it off Zion's Facebook page and hung it up last week.

Last week was when Manuel had given up any remaining hope of ever finding him alive. It'd been six months since he went missing. Virtually no one was ever found alive when they've been missing that long.

But while Manuel might have given up the hope of finding him alive, he had not given up on *finding him*. And, just as important, to him at least, finding whoever took the boy's life. Ever since hanging the picture, Manuel had looked at it every morning as a reminder of what they'd stolen.

He locked the door to his apartment (though any thief desperate enough to target it honestly deserved their meager spoils) and cast a glare across the parking lot to where his car was parked. Today was going to be a hot one. Even with the sun still well below the horizon, he could feel it in the air. Manuel lifted the collar of his shirt and gave himself a sniff to make sure he'd remembered to put on deodorant.

At least he wouldn't have to work outside in this heat. Today, in fact, Manuel didn't have to work at all. It was Friday, but Fridays were the first day of his weekend. He could have pulled rank and demanded a traditional weekend schedule if he'd wanted to, but Manuel didn't care enough. One day was the same as another to him; might as well let the football fans and churchgoers in the department have Sundays.

And the best part about having Fridays off was that most other people didn't. In a town like Hooper Valley and its population of 56,000, give or take, there weren't any lines in the stores or traffic clogging the roads on weekdays during work hours. Of course, that'd been changing a bit lately with so many folks working from home. Or not working at all. There seemed to be a lot of that going around lately too.

Wouldn't matter either way where he was headed, though; in all his years of going there, there wasn't a single time Manuel had ever seen the Yellow Dog Diner busy, weekday or not. It must have been a failure of marketing or location maybe, because the food sure wasn't to blame.

By the time he pulled into the Yellow Dog's parking lot, Manuel's stomach was starting to snarl. He scanned the lot for Phil King's blue Toyota and frowned when he didn't see it. The old fossil had better not make him wait again. If he did, Manuel was going to order without him. But halfway to the restaurant's entrance, he saw The Sheriff's pickup pull into the lot.

It might have been confusing for folks outside of Wayne County to hear anyone call Phil by that title. He could hardly walk anymore, and he looked more like a skeleton these days than a living, breathing man. Manuel figured the only reason Phil still had his driver's license was that there wasn't a cop in the state with the balls to take it from him. He'd retired nearly twenty years ago and passed the torch to Manuel, but that didn't matter none to anyone around here. Wayne County could go through a hundred more sheriffs, and Phil King would still be *The Sheriff.* In this little corner of the world, the man had a reputation bigger than Wyatt Earp's.

Manuel waited by the entrance for Phil to park and catch up. By the time he made it across the lot, Manuel was even hungrier.

"Go any slower and you're gonna start moving backward," Manuel said.

"I hope you have the misfortune of living as long as I have, Manny," Phil said. "Might make you regret all those smartass remarks."

"I kind of doubt I have to worry about it," Manuel said, holding the door open for him.

"Place is busy today," Phil said, surveying the small dining room. By the Yellow Dog Diner's standards, it was true; one of the tables and three of the booths were occupied. Including the booth Phil and Manuel always sat at.

There was a middle-aged couple sitting there now. If they were locals—which anyone who came here almost certainly was— they probably wouldn't hesitate to move tables for The Sheriff.

But Manuel picked out a booth a little closer to the entrance, and he and Phil sat down.

A waitress with wavy blonde hair came by their table almost as soon as they were settled. Kylie Hargrove was her name. Her pop used to work at the feed store on Gibbs Street.

"You guys getting the usual today?" she asked.

"Let me get sausage with mine this time, darling," Phil said.

"The usual for me," Manuel said.

"You got it," Kylie said. "I'll be right back with a pot of coffee."

Manuel watched Phil as he watched Kylie walk away. Even at eighty-two years old, The Sheriff still had an eye for the ladies.

"She's gonna catch you staring at her one of these days, you know?" he said.

"No law against lookin'."

"How's Mason doing?" Manuel asked. Mason, Phil's oldest son, had been diagnosed with liver cancer last month. From what Manuel understood, the prognosis wasn't good.

"Chemo's been kicking his ass. But he's keeping his head up."

"Here's that coffee for you," Kylie said, returning to their table with a stainless-steel pitcher.

Phil thanked her, then looked back to Manuel. "You talk to your sister yet?"

"No," Manuel said, in a tone he hoped would shut the topic down. Phil had been subtly pressuring him to mend things with her for several years. Ever since Zion went missing, he hadn't been so subtle about it.

"Family means something, Manny. Especially when shit goes south."

Manuel filled his mug to the brim with coffee from the pitcher and took his time stirring in the cream and sugar. Marissa didn't want to talk to him. Probably least of all now with everything she was going through. She would have called him by now if she did.

"How's the job treating you?" Phil asked.

"Same old same old."

"All kind of runs together eventually, doesn't it? I got a theory, no matter how exciting what you do for a livin' is, it still winds up getting old."

"The job ain't near as exciting as it was when you wore the badge anyway, Phil. It's a lot more paperwork and a lot less cracking skulls these days."

"I never cracked no skull that didn't deserve it," Phil said. "And I bet the ones that are still around would thank me for it if you asked 'em. Probably the only reason half of 'em are still around in the first place."

The food came a few minutes later, and neither of them talked for a while. One of the many things Manuel had in common with his former boss was that they were both serious about their food. But while anyone who looked at Manuel would know he didn't miss many meals, Phil had somehow stayed as lean and sinewy as he'd always been.

"You know," Phil said once his plate was clean, "I get the feeling there's more changed than just the job itself."

"How so?"

"The town's changed. The people. Hell, the whole damn world has. I don't envy you, Manny. I don't envy anyone who's gonna be around long enough to see how this thing ends."

"You think I'm gonna live to see the world end?" Manuel asked.

"Could be," Phil said, and left it at that.

"I have been getting this strange feeling lately," Manuel said.

"What kinda strange feeling?"

Manuel thought for a while about how to put it to words. "Like something's happening right in front of my nose, I guess. Something big. And I just can't see it."

Phil shrugged and took a sip of coffee. "Most cops don't make it very far if they ain't at least a little paranoid."

"I think there's more to it this time."

"Having a member of your family go missing is bound to make a person a bit paranoid too."

"So you're saying it's all in my head?"

"Not necessarily," Phil said. "But you've got to watch yourself either way. I've seen good men drive themselves mad over cases. Cases that don't even have anything to do with them personally, but they make it personal before it's all said and done. And if its personal right from the start, well…"

"Well what?"

"All I'm saying is that just 'cause you dive headfirst down the rabbit hole don't always mean you're gonna find the rabbit. And if you don't…find it, I mean…you better be sure you're strong enough to pull yourself back out again."

"Weren't you the one just talking about the world ending?" Manuel said. But he knew what The Sheriff was getting at. He'd seen it before himself. People in their profession, by nature, didn't like to let things go. They'd rather let it ruin them instead. "I'm not giving up on him yet, Phil."

"Not saying you should," Phil said. "So, have you found anything new?"

"Found some more people who saw the boys at the football game. No one knew anything helpful, though. There's security footage of them stopping at a gas station at 8:46 that night. That would have been just before they went to The Sapphire Lounge. Also not very helpful."

"What about their cell phones?"

"There aren't a lot of towers around here. Which means—"

"I know what it means," Phil interrupted with a touch of annoyance. "Means tracking the signal will tell you what county they were in, not what street they were standing on."

"Pretty much," Manuel said. "There's a ping at 11:13 p.m. that puts them somewhere south, southeast of Hooper Valley. Could've been five miles out of town, could've been twenty. There's nothing for almost three hours after that, then one more ping at 2:03 a.m. somewhere near Cunningham Park."

"So that would mean three college-aged boys went all that time without using their phones."

"It could mean a few things," Manuel said. "Their batteries could've run out of juice. They might have fallen asleep somewhere. Or—"

"Or someone took their phones to Cunningham Park and turned one of them on again before they dumped them to throw the cops off the trail."

"Phil, if you keep finishing my sentences for me, I'm just gonna sit back and let you do all the talkin'."

"Maybe you should start talkin' a little faster, Manny."

"Anyway…yeah. That's a possibility too."

"Tell me something," Phil said. "That area south of town the 11:13 ping put 'em at. Charlotte Mallory's place wouldn't happen to fall in that circle, would it?"

Manuel had told him about his visit to Ms. Mallory's the last time they were together, but still, it surprised him to hear Phil mention her again. "It's within the radius," he said.

"That woman's always rubbed me the wrong way. I tried reading one of her books one time, you know? About the most perverted piece of literature, if you want to call it that, I've ever laid eyes on. When you told me she was the last one to have seen them…well, it's something I ain't been able to stop thinking about."

"She's got a solid alibi."

"Her sister, right?"

"Yeah. Lilibeth Wyatt. Said she picked Charlotte up from The Sapphire Lounge about eleven and took her home. The bartender confirmed that Charlotte left her car there that night. Said she came back for it the next day."

"You remember what I said earlier? About family meaning something. Especially when shit goes south."

Manuel saw where Phil was leading him. Close friends and family could never be *too* solid of an alibi.

"It doesn't pass the sniff test anyway," he said. "Why would an attractive, successful woman want to abduct three college boys? And how could she pull it off if she did?"

"Don't ever underestimate a determined woman, Manny. And don't think they're all angels, neither. You ever hear of Aileen Wuornos?"

"It rings a bell."

"She murdered seven men down in Florida back in...1990, believe it was. Seven grown men in just one year's time."

"I hear you, Phil," Manuel said. "I already followed that trail as far as it would lead me, though. Would need a warrant to get any further. Takes a lot more than a bad feeling to get one of those signed, you know."

"I know there's a lot you can get done without them, too, if you're willing to treat a few rules like suggestions."

Manuel smirked, was about to say something about all the rules The Sheriff used to bend back in his day, when the phone in his pocket started to ring. Manuel pulled it out and saw his brother-in-law's name on the screen. He stared at it for a second; it'd been years since he'd seen that name on his phone. Then he gave Phil an "I need to take this" glance and answered the call.

"Hey, man," Ricky said. His baritone voice sounded mostly the same as it had the last time they'd spoke, but much sadder and more tired than ever before.

"What's going on, Ricky?" Manuel could feel his blood pressure rising. Whatever the reason for this call, it had to be something big.

"I thought you should know...umm..." Ricky sniffed and took a deep breath. It sounded like he'd either been crying or was on the verge of it.

"Talk to me," Manuel said.

"Marissa's in the hospital. She uh…she tried to kill herself, man."

"What hospital?" Manuel asked, already standing up from the booth.

"Trinity Valley Medical Center. In Dallas."

"I'll be there in a couple hours."

19

Nosocomephobia was a word Manuel had never heard before. But if told it meant a fear of hospitals, he could have diagnosed himself. He hated them. Always had ever since he'd been forced to spend three weeks in one as a kid following a severe allergic reaction.

The sterile floors and walls, the smell of antiseptic, the coughing and sniffling from the crowd in the waiting room—it hadn't taken long for all of these to make his head swim and his chest feel tight.

He probably looked like he needed to be admitted himself by the time he made it to the receptionist desk. The very idea of that made his stomach twist.

"I'm here to see Marissa Brooks," he said.

The receptionist—an older woman with thick-rimmed glasses and too much makeup—started typing at her computer. "And you are, sir?"

"Manuel Garcia. I'm her brother."

"I see. It says here Mrs. Brooks is still in ICU. You're welcome to visit her, but she might not be awake yet."

"That's fine." As much as anything, Manuel wanted away from this waiting room. An ICU room with its dim lights and whirring machines might not be much better, but at least he'd be away from all the contagious strangers.

"She's in room 5J," the receptionist said. "That's on the fifth floor. Elevators are down the hall on the right."

Manuel thanked her and headed down the hall, throttling his anxious pace just enough to not draw too much attention.

It took him a while to find the room once he'd made the elevator ride to the fifth floor. They built these places like a rat maze. But after a couple wrong turns, he found the right hallway and, eventually, the door marked 5J.

He stopped in front of it, decided he should knock, and rapped gently against the wood so as to not disturb his sister if she was sleeping. A few seconds later, Ricky opened the door.

"Come in," he said under his breath. "She's resting right now."

Manuel stepped into the room and eased the door closed. The curtains on the far side of the room were pulled, but there was enough sunlight getting in for him to see Marissa lying in the railed bed near the room's center. Her eyes were closed, a few tresses of dark, matted hair draped over them. There was an IV in her hand connected to a bag on a silver stand. Then Manuel saw why the doctors had put it there and not the forearm like normal—both of Marissa's arms were wrapped from elbow to wrist in thick bandages.

"She lost a lot of blood," Ricky whispered, catching him looking. "They had to give her a transfusion. Gave her twelve units. I guess that's a lot, according to the doctor."

"Is she…"

"They think she'll make it. The worst is over now. But they've got to keep an eye on her still. Doc says there could be complications."

"How are you doing, Ricky?" Manuel asked.

The answer was obvious. Both of them knew it. But Ricky still fought to keep a stiff lip. "Oh…you know. I'm making it too." He sat down then in one of the cushioned chairs next to Marissa's bed. There was a second chair next to it, and he motioned to it. "Might as well take a seat, man. They gave her a sedative about thirty minutes ago. I'm thinking she's gonna be out a while."

Manuel hoped she would be. She needed her rest. And, truth be told, the idea of speaking with her again made him almost as anxious as these hospital walls.

"Let me ask you something, Ricky," he said after he'd taken a seat. "And I want you to be honest with me. Is it alright that I'm here? You know…I mean, with how it's been between us. The last thing I want is to upset her."

"Manny, I wouldn't have called you if I didn't want you to come. She needs you now. It's time to let bygones be bygones."

Manuel nodded. It was the only respectful thing to do. But some bygones weren't so easy to forgive and forget. Marissa blamed him for the death of their father. And, in a way, she was right.

"She did forgive you, I think," Ricky said. He must have seen the doubt all over Manuel's face. "I think she was just afraid, or too proud maybe, to be the one to reach out first. And me…well, the way I've always seen it, it wasn't really your fault."

Manuel didn't exactly see it that way himself, though. Six years ago, he had been living with his father, Pedro, after Violet kicked him out of the house. One night, Pedro collapsed on the bathroom floor. Manuel had been drinking—he'd always been drinking those days—and was absolutely shitfaced when it happened.

He could have called an ambulance. That would have been the best thing to do. But that's not what he did. Manuel had relived that night a thousand times, and he still couldn't say what he'd been thinking. He guessed he must have thought he could get them there faster than an ambulance would.

Where he actually got them was stuck up to the doors in a ditch not a mile down the highway. Manuel had panicked then. He'd mashed the accelerator so hard the spinning tires sent a spray of mud ten feet in the air. When that didn't work, he'd got out and pushed hard enough to stretch a muscle in his back. And all the while, the cell phone sitting in his pocket never crossed his drunken mind.

A neighbor found them a half hour later. Then the call was finally made. But by then, it was already too late. When the paramedics got there, it was a corpse they put on the stretcher.

Why neither of them had called in his car being buried in the ditch, Manuel still didn't know. There's no way they could have missed the glaze in his eyes or how he slurred his words. Maybe he got a pass because he was the sheriff. Manuel didn't like to think that was true, but he knew it was the way the world worked sometimes. Or maybe they both just decided not to add to the misery of a recent divorcee who'd just lost his dad. Manuel didn't like that theory much either, but he supposed pity was a more palatable reason than privilege.

"Thank you for calling me," he said, while the monitor by Marissa's bed continued to beep loud and rhythmically.

"Yeah," Ricky said. "For sure."

Minutes passed. Both of them sat silent, watching Marissa sleep. When Manuel looked over at Ricky, he could see the tears he'd been fighting back finally starting to well in his eyes.

"I thought I was gonna lose her, Manny. The blood…I thought for sure she was gone."

"You saved her life," Manuel said. "A lot of people would have panicked."

"I can't help thinking what it's gonna be like when they send her home. I'm gonna be scared all the time she might try it again. She's been in a bad place lately. Unless our boy comes walking through the door someday, I don't know if it's ever gonna get better."

"I'm going to find him, Ricky. One way or another."

In fact, the more he thought about it, the more he realized how senseless it was for him to be here. Whether she forgave him or not, Marissa didn't want to see him. She wanted to see her son—or at a very bare minimum, to know what happened to him. Manuel could only imagine the way the questions tortured her. If his instincts were true and it was too late to bring him back alive, he could at least give her answers.

"I think I'm gonna go," Manuel said. He thought Ricky might try and talk him into staying, but he only nodded. "Tell her I came by whenever she wakes up. Tell her…tell her I said I love her, and I'll see her soon."

"Yeah, Manny. I'll tell her."

If they'd both been standing, Manuel might have hugged his brother-in-law. He wasn't normally the hugging type, figured Ricky probably wasn't either, but it seemed then like the thing to do. Instead, he gave him a pat on the shoulder.

Manuel stopped next to Marissa's bed on the way out of the room, even though the urge to be out of this awful place and get back to the only useful thing he could do was strong. He gently touched her face and was glad to feel it warm against his hand despite how pale she looked.

"I will find him," Manuel whispered so quietly he doubted either she or Ricky actually heard. But he was speaking to himself more than them anyway. "I promise."

20

Zion stared at the back cover of the book in his hands and blinked a few times, thinking maybe he was hallucinating. He'd heard before of seeing people's faces pop up in random places when those people haunt your thoughts—and no one haunted his thoughts more than The Bitch.

But when he swiped his thumb across the postage-stamp-sized image at the bottom of the of the book's back cover, it didn't wipe away or disappear like he expected it to.

It was *her*. Charlotte Mallory, apparently. And if he needed any more convincing, the bio above the photo sealed the deal.

"*Charlotte Mallory is the author of more than a dozen* New York Times *Best Sellers in the dark romance genre, including* Torched Hearts, Sins of the Flesh, *and* Tempting the Devil. *She lives on a ranch outside of Hooper Valley, Texas, where she enjoys taking care of her animals, nature photography, and writing twisted love stories.*"

Hooper Valley. Much of that night over five months ago— the night The Bitch kidnapped them—was a blur now, but Zion remembered that name clearly. It was the name of the town he and his friends had been visiting. The one they met her in.

And this was The Bitch's book. Zion turned it over and examined the front cover. It was a copy of *Tempting the Devil*. The art showed a shirtless man with chiseled abs and coal-black hair. Small match flames of fire burned in his pupils, and the smoke rising from them seemed to form a pair of horns on either side of his head.

Zion shot a glance at the cardboard box he'd pulled the book from. The Bitch…*Charlotte Mallory*…had brought it down about an hour ago. A fresh supply of reading material that had interested him just enough to riffle through the stack until he spotted the one with her picture on it.

He wondered if she'd meant to include it or if it had ended up there by accident. He guessed it was an accident; for whatever reason, she'd never revealed her name or any other personal details, even though Zion already knew more than enough to have cops at her door in an hour if he ever escaped. It seemed strange that she'd reveal it all now, and in this way.

Which meant what he needed now was a place to hide the book. That way, if it was an accident, she wouldn't see it and take it away. Zion scanned the perimeter of the basement his chain would let him reach, then decided the couch cushions were his best bet.

He slid the book under the cloth cushion, stood up and looked it over, then, satisfied there wouldn't be any noticeable bulge, pulled the book out again.

He flipped it open and read the dedication. Charlotte thanked her fans, her editor, and her agent. No mention of any friends or family, but that didn't surprise Zion. Those were usually in short supply for crazy, murderous bitches.

He looked at the stairway and made sure the basement door was still closed, despite knowing it would be; for the most part, her visits came on a pretty reliable schedule. Then he sat down on the couch and put the book in his lap.

He wondered what he was really doing. What it was he hoped to accomplish. It felt good to learn The Bitch's name. Learning those intimate details she'd tried to keep hidden from him felt like getting one over on her. But as for actually reading the book, he couldn't see how that would help him any more than reading *Misery* or *Dune* or any of the others in the box. And they at least were a lot more his style.

Then a quote came to him. He'd probably heard it in a movie or seen it on a meme, but he knew where it came from originally. It was from Sun Tzu's *Art of War*.

Know your enemy.

It wasn't like he had anything better to do anyway. So, Zion flipped the book open to a random chapter near the middle and started to read.

Tempting the Devil: Chapter 21

Hazel slammed her front door closed and flipped the deadbolt. Her legs, which had felt like Jello the entire sprint up her driveway, finally gave out, and she slid down with her back against the door until she hit the hardwood floor.

She'd seen something she wasn't meant to. Something she could never unsee. She'd always known Blake Christianson was not a safe man. In a world where "golden retriever boyfriends" had become all the rage, Blake was a rottweiler.

And yet...and yet, somehow, she had never imagined him actually hurting anyone. He'd always been so gentle with her, so professional with his associates. Even though the dark streak in him was wide and clear to see, she had never seen him let it loose.

But there'd been a sack over that man's head. He'd been begging for his life while Blake and Rocco dragged him to the woods at the back of the estate. And as Hazel stood there in the driveway, hiding behind Blake's Escalade with a bottle of wine in her trembling hands, she'd heard the shot.

She'd run away then. Ran all the way to a Shell station two miles away and called a cab from there.

She wondered if he'd seen her. Probably not, but it didn't matter. He'd know either way as soon as they spoke again. There was no way she'd be able to hide it from him.

Her phone buzzed then, and Hazel's heart leapt into her throat. But it was just a random notification. Blake rarely texted her. When he wanted to talk, he either called or just showed up.

It was fine for him. But her showing up like she had, unexpected...that had been a mistake. She should have known better. You don't sneak up on the dangerous ones. Do and you might be the one who gets surprised.

Hazel's phone buzzed again. This time, it was a text. From Stephanie, not Blake.

"We need to meet up again," the text read. Then, another a second later, "I need to show you something."

No telling what she'd dug up on Blake now. Sometimes Hazel hated that her friend was an attorney with investigative skills outdone only by her nosiness. Whatever she'd found, it couldn't be worse than what Hazel already knew.

Blake Christianson had murdered a man. And it likely wasn't his first.

Hazel started to correct herself, to allow herself to take comfort in the idea that Blake probably wasn't the one who pulled the trigger. That probably would've been Rocco's job.

Probably or not, though, it definitely didn't matter. Blake was the one who gave the order. In the eyes of God and the courts alike, he was guilty of murder.

It was time for Hazel to start facing these cold, hard facts. No more slipping on the blinders anytime the topic of how the Christianson family built their empire came up. She'd been caught up in a whirlwind of luxury, mystery, and passion ever since the day Blake walked into her boutique, but now it was decision time.

Deal or no deal, with her soul on the table.

She could leave him. He wouldn't try and stop her. At least she didn't think he would. Or she could decide not to care what crimes he committed. She couldn't pretend anymore not to see the blood that dripped from his money. But what she could do was stare right at it and never blink.

A shudder passed through her, then her thoughts went to the bottle of wine still in her hand. She stood up on shaky legs and went to find a corkscrew.

So, this was what losing your soul felt like. It happened so much quicker than she ever could have guessed. Twenty-five years of life spent considering herself a "good person," and here she was now, considering trading all her morals for a man who four intoxicating months ago had been a stranger.

Having at last managed to uncork the bottle, Hazel poured—

Zion heard the basement door unlocking. He closed the book and rushed to slide it underneath the couch cushion. Just as he'd resumed a natural pose on the couch, the door opened, and he heard The Bitch's hurried footsteps coming down the stairs.

She stopped when she reached the bottom. Stopped and stared at him. Zion just stared back.

"I think…" she said. She took a bite at the corner of her lip. "I might have brought a book down here by accident."

"You brought a whole bunch of them down," Zion said, glancing at the cardboard box sitting near the foot of the couch.

"Can you actually slide that back over to me?"

Zion let out an impatient sigh. All for show; on the inside, his heart was racing. But he'd always been good at keeping a calm exterior. You don't get to play quarterback for the varsity team as a freshman unless you're cool under pressure.

He aimed the box, then gave it a hard push. It slid across the floor and stopped a couple of feet in front of The Bitch. He watched as she bent over and started taking the books out one by one, wondering how long it would take for her to realize the one she was looking for wasn't there. And, more importantly, wondering what she'd do when she did.

When all the books in the box were out on the floor, Charlotte studied them like they were puzzle pieces. Then she shot a look at Zion. Zion raised his eyebrows a little.

"Did you…" She closed her mouth again and frowned. "You know what, never mind."

She put the books back in the box, seeming in a rush, then slid it back to within Zion's reach. Zion watched it come to a stop, smiled, and even laughed a little. "You really are crazy, aren't you?"

The Bitch didn't answer. She was taillights already, halfway back up the stairs by the time he got the words out. But Zion kept smiling anyway. That part wasn't an act. He didn't know the reason—and it likely amounted to nothing—but there was a reason she didn't want him to have that book. And that instantly made it his most prized possession in the world.

Charlotte knew as soon as she saw the name on her buzzing cell phone that it wasn't good news. Her sister never called her anymore unless there was some kind of trouble.

She thought about ignoring it. Letting it wait until some other time when Malachi wasn't bouncing off the walls and she was operating on more than a couple hours of sleep. But ignoring trouble wasn't wise.

"Hey," she said, sitting down on the sofa as she answered the call. Odds were this was going to be an "are you sitting down?" type of conversation. Might as well get ahead of the curve.

"He came by here again," Lilibeth said. Charlotte couldn't decide whether she sounded more frightened or angry.

"Who?" Charlotte asked, though she figured she already knew the answer.

"Who do you think, Charlotte? It was that sheriff friend of yours."

"What did he want?"

"He wanted to grill me for forty-five minutes is what he wanted. I thought he was going to make a pallet on the floor and stay the night."

"Why didn't you tell him to leave?"

A brief pause. "You can do that?"

"Yeah, Lils. You can do that."

"Whatever. I'm sick of it, Charlotte. I don't know what you did this time, and I don't want to. But I'm done covering for you. I couldn't even sleep last night, I was so anxious. And guilt ridden. I'm not doing it anymore."

"I'm sorry," Charlotte said. "I won't ask you to."

Unless she had to, that is. Prison, even a death sentence, didn't frighten her. But she'd do anything to keep Malachi safe. And, to a lesser extent, to keep the world safe from him.

"You better mean that. I don't care about the money anymore, Charlotte. Whatever it is you're caught up in, I want nothing more to do with it."

She hung up before Charlotte could respond. Probably a good thing, because Charlotte didn't have a good response to give her.

There had been two occasions, both taking place at The Sapphire Lounge, where Charlotte screwed up. Both times she'd been desperate, in a rush to capture someone before Malachi grew impatient enough to do it himself, and both times involved breaking her cardinal rule of not hunting close to home. The lie she'd asked Lilibeth to tell had been the same both times also: she was supposed to say she picked Charlotte up at The Sapphire Lounge and drove her home alone.

But Charlotte had never told Lilibeth *why*, and she'd been smart enough not to ask. The two of them had always had each other's back. The check Charlotte had handed her the first time she asked Lilibeth to lie on her behalf no doubt helped too. Her husband JD had lost his job around that time, and Charlotte got the sense they were in trouble. She would have helped out even if she hadn't needed Lilibeth's help in return. She wondered if Lilibeth would have done the same. But, then again, what she'd asked of Lilibeth was much greater than a bit of money Charlotte wouldn't miss.

Charlotte woke her phone up again and checked the time. It had been a while since she checked in on Malachi. Though he was always well-behaved during the first few weeks following a feeding, she still didn't like to leave him alone for long.

On her way up the stairs, Charlotte tried to imagine (for the thousandth time) what would happen if she told Lilibeth the truth. Part of her longed to, if for no other reason than to get the burden off her chest. As if sharing her terrible secret with even a single other soul might make it a little less crushing.

It was hard to picture how her sister would take it. And it didn't matter anyway. The risk outweighed the reward so heavily that Charlotte could never tell her—or anyone—no matter how badly she wanted to.

Charlotte put it from her mind, then eased open the door to Malachi's bedroom. She spotted him on the floor, playing with his Legos.

"Whatcha building?" she asked, sitting down beside him.

"A spaceship," Malachi said. Charlotte looked at the asymmetrical clump of blocks he was working on and smiled. NASA would've had concerns, but she wasn't about to raise any.

"Wow. A spaceship, huh? Where's it gonna go?"

"It's going to space, Momma," Malachi said, looking up from his work to scrunch his eyebrows at her like she was slow in the head.

Charlotte reached out and mussed up his hair. "You're a mess, you know it?"

"I'm going to build it this big," Malachi said, stretching out his arms as far as he could—a wingspan that a lot of basketball players would have been jealous of. "Big enough for me to ride. For real, I mean."

"For real?" Charlotte said in mock amazement. "Now why would you want to go to outer space, kiddo? It's pretty cold and dark up there, you know?"

Malachi shrugged. "I want to see things."

"What kind of things?"

Another shrug. "New things. New places."

Charlotte put both arms around him and pulled him into her lap. She stroked his head while he looked up at her. And the hint of sadness she saw in his eyes made her feel like crying. She'd known it was inevitable, the loneliness and longing that would awaken in him someday. And there was nothing she could do to fix it.

"It isn't safe out there, baby. I know it isn't always fun staying here all the time. But you're just too special for this world, Malachi. It would not treat you kindly."

"I don't think I'd get hurt, Momma," Malachi said.

He was probably right. Malachi had never suffered a serious injury in his seven years of life, but the small cuts and bruises he did sustain always healed at a remarkable rate. She couldn't remember the last time he'd been sick more than a day, and his reserves of stamina were bottomless as far as she could tell. In time, he might very well prove invulnerable to anything the world could throw at him. For its sake, that only made her more determined to keep him by her side.

"Can I help?" Charlotte asked, twisting one of the blocks between her fingers.

Malachi rubbed his chin. "Wanna build an alien spaceship and have a battle?"

"I would *love* to build an alien spaceship, kiddo."

For the next hour, they played together. Charlotte did her best to make the whole thing educational, talking about the moon landing and the different planets while they worked on their designs. One of so many things that Malachi had missed by spending his life on this ranch was a real education. Charlotte wasn't sure how much it would ultimately matter; it wasn't like he had to prepare for a future career. But, still, she refused to allow her son to grow up ignorant of the world he lived in.

"Hey, Momma?" Malachi said as they worked on putting the Legos back in their plastic bin.

"Hey what?"

"Could a spaceship get all the way to Heaven?"

Charlotte smiled. "I don't think so. I think Heaven is pretty far away."

Far away from this world, that's for sure, Charlotte thought. She had taught Malachi about Heaven because the idea of it had comforted her when she was his age. But she wasn't sure she still believed in it anymore.

"Is that where Daddy is?" Malachi asked.

Charlotte kept smiling. On the outside at least. On the inside, she felt cold dread at the mere mention of that man.

"Yes, baby," she said, even though it was a lie. It had been easier to tell Malachi that his father had passed away than to try and explain the truth. But she had no real reason to believe that he was dead. Even if he was dead—and if Heaven was real—that's not where he'd be.

"What was he like?"

Charlotte took a long breath in. It wasn't the first time Malachi had asked this question, in some form or another. But as he grew, the answer she gave had to grow along with him. Even if it, too, was more lies than truth.

"Your father was a very powerful man," Charlotte started as Malachi watched her, entranced.

Then she told him a story of how they met. Not the real one, but the version he could understand. The version that was best for him to believe.

"Did you know that Momma used to clean people's houses for her job? Well, your father hired me to clean his and…"

2 2

Charlotte winced as the large, ornate door slammed in her face. She stood on the porch for a moment staring at it, tempted to knock and give the old hag who'd just closed it a piece of her mind.

Money couldn't buy manners, that was for sure. Quite the opposite, in Charlotte's experience. But it could buy influence, and that meant she couldn't afford to piss off Mrs. Allen any more than she already had. No telling how many of Charlotte's existing—and potential—clients in the area were friends of hers.

"I know you took it," Mrs. Allen had said. The words still rang in Charlotte's ears. A tennis bracelet was what she'd been talking about. One Charlotte couldn't have afforded to rent for a day. It had apparently gone missing after Charlotte's last cleaning.

But she wasn't the only one who'd been in that house while Mrs. Allen was away. Her parasite of a twenty-eight-year-old son lived there too. From the residue that always seemed to be on his upper lip, he loved either powdered donuts or a powdery something else with a passion. Mrs. Allen probably truly believed it was the former, if she ever even noticed.

It wouldn't have done Charlotte a bit of good to try and turn the accusation on him, though. Mrs. Allen's grown-ass baby boy could do no wrong.

The more Charlotte thought about it, the angrier she got. She stormed across the long, flagstone walkway to her car and flung open the door. It was hot today, and even hotter inside the car. It made the warmth rising in her face even more intense.

She buckled her seat belt and put the key in the ignition. Maybe she'd peel out and leave skid marks on the bitch's immaculate driveway. But no, Charlotte thought, there again was that pesky thing called reputation to think of. And Charlotte doubted her old Camry's sputtering engine could muster the pep to burn rubber anyway.

She turned the key then. And her heart sank into her stomach. The sound that followed wasn't that of her engine turning over but the rapid click-click-click-click-click of her worst nightmare at this moment: a dead battery.

It had been on the fritz for a while now. It needed to be replaced, but who knew the damn things were so expensive. Walking out of that AutoZone because she didn't have enough cash in her pocket had been embarrassing, and she'd been whistling past the graveyard ever since. But now the timing could not possibly be worse.

Charlotte pressed her head against the steering wheel, accidentally bumping the horn, then jerked back, even more mortified now that Mrs. Allen was surely watching from behind her satin curtains.

She ran through her options but quickly realized there was only one—no matter how much she hated it. She opened the car door, slammed it closed without meaning to, and began her walk of shame back across the driveway.

Mrs. Allen looked exactly like Charlotte expected her to when she answered the door—her painted lips pursed and her gold-rimmed glasses resting on the tip of her hooked nose as she stared down it at the peasant on her porch.

"Car trouble?" she asked, her voice dripping with disdain.

"It's the battery," Charlotte said.

"You should buy yourself a new one, dear."

"I'm going to. As soon as I can get to the auto shop."

"No, I mean a new car. That bracelet you stole is worth more than any car you've ever owned, I can promise you that."

"I..." Charlotte resisted the instinct to defend herself. Kept her eyes on her shoes. "Do you have jumper cables I could use?"

Mrs. Allen scoffed. "Sure, dear. I keep them in the curio cabinet right next to the crystal."

Your son knows a thing or two about crystal, I bet, Charlotte thought but bit her tongue.

"Can I use your phone then?" Another pitiful request, but hers had died about an hour ago. Batteries just had it out for her today, it seemed.

Mrs. Allen's lips puckered even tighter. It looked like she'd bitten into a lemon wedge. "I don't think it would be very wise to let you and your sticky fingers back into my home."

Charlotte showed no emotion, but she imagined what it would feel like to take those sticky fingers of hers and jam them deep into the woman's reptile eyes. Make them sticky for real.

"Wait here," Mrs. Allen said. "I'll give the groundskeeper a call. And only because I don't want your car cluttering up my driveway. Otherwise, I'd make you walk home and call the police to come have it removed."

She closed the door then. Charlotte heard its lock turn, then the sound of her footsteps stamping away.

It crossed Charlotte's mind for the first time to wonder why she hadn't called the police in the first place, if she really believed that Charlotte had taken the bracelet. She considered that maybe Mrs. Allen knew—or at least suspected—the truth about her son after all, and this brought Charlotte a twinge of satisfaction.

Minutes passed. Charlotte started to think that maybe that lock turning had been more than just another jab. Maybe Mrs. Allen had no intention of calling anyone to help her.

But then she spotted someone at the end of the drive, standing near the stone and wrought iron gate at the estate's entrance. It must be the groundskeeper, she thought at first. Before she realized what he was wearing.

He was a little too far away for her to see clearly—God forbid Victoria Allen not have the longest drive in her neighborhood—but it looked like he was wearing a suit and vest. And a jacket too. A strange choice for anyone on a day this sweltering, but the kind of thing you'd never see a groundskeeper wearing unless it was their wedding or their funeral.

Something shiny dangled from his hand, and he twirled it back and forth. It caught the sunlight and sent a scatter of dazzling rays in her direction.

She squinted to see what the man looked like and realized he was looking her direction too. Staring right at her, it seemed. He lifted his arm and waved at her, slow and dramatic, with the shiny strand still dangling from his fingers. A little dazed, Charlotte waved back.

A flash of sunlight from the object in his hand caught her directly in the eye, blinding her for a dazzling instant. And when it was gone, so too was the man standing near the gate. Charlotte blinked, drowning in disbelief. He might have been far away, but she'd clearly seen him standing there.

Her throat tightened a little. Maybe all those hours spent breathing in cleaning chemicals and slaving away for rich, entitled snobs had finally gotten to her. Maybe she was cracking.

She stared at the gate for a while longer, half expecting the man in the suit to reappear any moment like the finale to a magic trick. But then the gate rolled open, and a white pickup truck pulled into the estate.

The driver parked next to Charlotte's car and got out, his t-shirt and grass-stained blue jeans making him a lot easier to place than the man in the suit.

"My name's Jimmy," the man said. "Mrs. Allen says you're having some car trouble."

"Yeah..." Charlotte said, trailing off for a moment. "Dead battery."

"Well, that's an easy enough fix at least," Jimmy said, reaching into the bed of his truck to grab a pair of red and black cables.

"Hey, was there a man..." She trailed off again.

"What's that?"

"Never mind."

Jimmy looked at her and scratched his beard. "You wanna pop your hood for me?"

Charlotte did. A couple minutes later, when Jimmy asked her to turn the key, the engine sputtered and hummed to life.

"I wouldn't kill it until you get to where you're going," Jimmy said. Charlotte thanked him and drove away.

By the time Charlotte made it up the metal stairs to the third floor of her apartment building, it was starting to get dark. She'd driven around for a while, listening to the radio to clear her head. What she'd expected to be an afternoon of mopping and scrubbing had turned to a whirlwind of events that still had her spinning.

When she reached the door, she checked the knob to make sure it was locked before she inserted her key. It was something she'd been doing ever since coming home one night last month to find her previous apartment robbed. The new one was in a slightly better area (and priced accordingly, unfortunately), but the habit still stuck.

She turned on the lights and tried not to let the state of disarray they revealed bring her down even more. For a housekeeper, she didn't keep a very clean house. But isn't that what they say about every profession? It's like how most chefs eat takeout and most truckers aren't fans of road trips; no one enjoys doing what they do for a living in their spare time.

Especially when they hate it with every ounce of their being. Few children, if any, dream of cleaning other people's houses when they grow up. And while Charlotte's upbringing in the Texas foster system had done a good job of keeping childhood dreams in check, she had still always longed for more.

She had only one ticket to get there, though, as far as she could see. And it might as well have been a lottery ticket. The odds were about the same.

Still, once she'd taken off her shoes and put her purse away, Charlotte headed straight for the laptop she'd left open on her kitchen table. There were worlds saved on it. Worlds of words and punctuations she had created one keystroke at a time. Three of them, in fact, and another still in the womb. So far, she hadn't been able to get anyone else to care about them. Certainly not the agents and publishers she'd been emailing relentlessly for the past five years.

Sometimes she wished she'd been born with some other passion and talent. If she'd been gifted at math, maybe she could have been a scientist or an engineer. Or a doctor with a boat and a lake house, if she'd been touched with a talent for medicine. But writing stories only paid the bills for a fortunate few, and Charlotte was rarely one whom fortune shone on.

She'd always made up for it as best she could with hard work. And that was the plan for tonight too; she figured she could get at least three or four hours of writing in before her eyelids grew too heavy.

Weaving around the moving boxes she had yet to unpack (it had only been three weeks, she consoled herself), Charlotte crossed her small living room and entered the even smaller kitchen. She felt at the wall for a moment, the location of the switch not yet fully committed to memory, and turned on the kitchen light.

She was already halfway seated at the table, ready to flip open her Chromebook and dive into some other, better world, when the sparkle caught her eye—a beam of rainbow fire that stopped her breath.

Sitting on top of her laptop was a diamond bracelet. A tennis bracelet, to be precise—white gold with diamonds the size of pencil erasers. Charlotte gaped at it, not daring to touch it. Her mind racing, it took her several moments to notice the piece of paper tucked underneath the bracelet.

This, she did pick up.

IF YOU'RE GOING TO SUFFER THE PUNISHMENT, MIGHT AS WELL ENJOY THE SPOILS.

With the bright overhead light shining straight through the thin piece of paper, Charlotte could see that there was writing on the other side as well. She flipped it over and found an address, written in the same scrawling style and blood-red ink.

1401 EAST BRADFORD. PRESTON HOLLOW, TEXAS.

Charlotte knew that neighborhood. It was a part of the city that even the likes of Victoria Allen couldn't afford to step foot in.

But how much money did it take to walk through walls? Because none of the windows were broken, and the only door into her apartment had not been breached either. It chilled her then, thinking of someone walking about her home. Placing the bracelet and the note on her table, then vanishing just as inexplicably as they'd appeared.

Charlotte reached for her phone, intent on calling the police, but she'd forgotten about it being dead. The charger was in her bedroom. Just a few minutes was all it would take, and she'd have enough juice to place the call. But instead of going for it, she let her fingers stray to the bracelet. The metal felt cold against her skin. Wrong to the touch. And yet the way those diamonds caught the light seemed to spark in her a fire just as brilliant.

Charlotte knew then, somewhere deep down, exactly how this was going to go. She'd always been a sucker for a good mystery. Just like she'd always been someone with precious little to lose.

She slipped the note into her pocket. Then the bracelet behind it. She took her phone, plugged it into the charger on her nightstand, then sat down on the edge of the bed and waited.

She wasn't going to call the police. Now that she'd calmed down a bit, the idea of getting them involved no longer interested her. What did interest her was the note.

And to unravel that mystery, she was going to need her GPS.

2 3

"Let's go! Let's go!" Zion shouted. His offensive line scrambled to get set while on the scoreboard clock, precious seconds ticked away. The center, a fellow senior named Miles Jones, gripped the football with a taped hand, and Zion crouched behind him. "Set, hike!"

Miles snapped the ball. Zion dropped back, scanning the waterlogged field through the bars of his face mask and the stream of rain that had been falling hard ever since the start of the second quarter. Before him, an orchestrated chaos unfolded. Receivers flew down the field with defenders glued to their hips. A blitzing middle linebacker smashed into the line, fighting to get through to Zion.

He saw his running back, Chase White, come open on a flat route, but Zion looked away from him. That completion would only get them a few yards. With seconds to go before halftime and their team down twenty-one points already, what they needed was a touchdown.

Then he saw it. Number 82—a sophomore with track-star wheels named Josh Daniels—had beat his man and was streaking toward the end zone, waving his hand over his head to get Zion's attention. Zion's heart skipped a beat, and he reared back his arm to make the pass.

But before he could release the ball, a collision from his blind side drove him into the ground and forced the breath from his lungs. He hit the muddy turf hard, sandwiched between it and two-hundred-some-odd pounds of defensive lineman lying on top of him.

Through the ringing in his ears, Zion heard the horn sounding the end of the first half. A sack was the one thing they couldn't afford, and now they'd missed their opportunity.

He let Miles help him up, then followed the team and coaches into the tunnel that led to their locker room. Two hours ago, they'd stormed out of this tunnel like the real-life versions of their bison mascot. The walk back in, though, was a lot less enthusiastic.

Zion sat down on one of the locker room benches. He put his helmet between his feet and his face in his hands. He had started all four years as the Trinity View Bisons quarterback, so he'd been here before—down big, getting his ass handed to him. But tonight was different. This was a playoff game. Win or go home. And he was a senior. One with no scholarship offers from any colleges, at that. Lose this game and he'd probably never put on the pads again.

Looking around the locker room, he could see the same realization setting in on the faces of the rest of the seniors. That hurt even worse. The thought of letting them down, making them feel the same pain he dreaded for himself, made Zion's throat tight.

"Listen up!" Coach Woods shouted. He wore a Trinity View windbreaker and clenched a clipboard so tightly in his hand it looked like he might splinter it. "I want every damn one of you to look at me and stop your sulking right now. You hear me?"

"Yes, Coach," every player in the room responded. But it had been timid enough that Zion could've predicted what came next.

"Get that weak shit out of here. I asked if you heard me."

"Yes, Coach!"

"There's still a whole half to be played," Coach Woods said. "We're down a bit. We got a hole to climb out of, okay? But I don't care if we're down a hundred, I'm not going to sit here and watch you all give up. You don't ever give up on yourselves, and you don't ever give up on family. That's what this team is. Family. And by God, I expect you to go out there and fight like it."

As far as halftime speeches went, it was pretty standard fare. Yet Zion would be lying if he said Coach Woods's fiery delivery didn't get his blood pumping a little harder. Looking around the locker room, it hit him how true those words had been. These were his brothers. Some of them he may never see again once the school year was over, but it didn't change that fact. Win or lose tonight, he was going to fight like hell for them.

The sound of the basement door opening stirred Zion from his dream. Slowly at first, its landscape dissolved before his eyes. Footsteps coming down the stairs brought him fully awake. Having grown used to The Bitch's comings and goings, it didn't startle him. Not at first, anyway. Not until he noticed the book lying open on his lap.

He thought about scrambling to hide it, but it was already too late. He could hear her at the bottom of the stairs. There was nothing to do now but roll with it. Try and get as much leverage out of the situation as he could, whatever that looked like.

Like most of her trips down here, The Bitch hardly even looked in his direction. For a moment, it seemed she might not even notice the book. But he saw her glance in his direction, start to turn away, then do a double take. She stared for a while at the book on his lap. Zion sat up and closed it.

"Where did you get that?" she asked.

"Umm…you brought it to me," Zion said, purposefully looking at her like she'd lost her mind. He wasn't sure where he was going with this yet, but any opportunity to mess with her head was one worth taking. And the gears in his own head were spinning a plan into place by the moment.

The Bitch opened her mouth to speak, then quickly closed it again. He could see what she was trying to calculate: whether he knew already that the book was hers. "I'm going to need that one back," she finally said.

Zion shrugged. "Come and get it."

The threat beneath this must have been more evident than he'd meant for it to be. Zion saw her eyes narrow. Saw her expression turn grave. "Do I need to remind you what would happen to you if—"

"No," Zion interjected. "You don't. I would die. Except we both know that's what's gonna happen anyway, so…"

"Slide it over to me," she said. Zion noticed that she stood just on the edge of where his chain would reach. Ever since Clint was taken away, she'd been careful to never cross the line. Like she'd seen, or at least anticipated, the change that'd come over him.

He thought for a bit about whether he should give the book back. But if she wanted it bad enough, she'd surely find some way to get it from him. He'd already read most of it, anyway. Already learned everything he could—which was never going to be much.

In fact, there was only one takeaway from it even worth taking away: The Bitch had a heart. She believed in love. No one could write about it the way she did if they didn't. Not unless she sold her soul for the ability—something Zion wouldn't put past her.

"I'll ask nicely one more time," she said.

Zion snorted, but he set the book down on the floor and gave it a hard shove. It went skittering across the cement and stopped right at her feet.

"It was pretty boring anyway," he said. He looked for some reaction from her, but she didn't flinch. She bent down and picked up the book, then turned sharply and headed back for the stairs, whatever task she'd come down here for in the first place apparently abandoned.

"Hey, Charlotte," Zion said when she was about halfway there. That stopped her in her tracks. "I know you wrote it."

She turned around and glared at him, but with more curiosity—or suspicion at most—than anger.

"I don't see what the big secret is, anyway," Zion said. "So you write books. How's that change anything?"

"You know my name now," she said.

Zion laughed a little and shook his head. "Yeah. That's true. And I also know what you look like. And where you live. And none of it even matters, because I'm never getting out of here."

"There's power in a name."

"There's power in the truth, too, Charlotte," Zion said, his tone full of pleading now. "So why don't you just tell it to me? If I already know all the rest of that stuff, what difference does it make?"

To his surprise, she actually seemed to consider this. He could see the uncertainty on her face. And when she finally spoke, her words seemed sincere for perhaps the first time since he had met her.

"If I told you the truth, you wouldn't believe it."

"Try me," Zion said. But it was no use. He could see it already.

"I'm sorry," she said. As hard as it was to accept, this seemed sincere as well.

She was gone before Zion could think of what to say next. Back up the stairs, bolting the door behind her, as if he had any chance of ever reaching it anyway with the chain around his leg.

Zion sighed and fell back onto the couch. His thoughts raced through a thousand possibilities of what she'd left unsaid. None of them made any sense, but that probably meant he was on the right track. Nothing about him being here, chained in a famous author's basement, made a bit of sense.

Two weeks ago, when Clint was taken away, Zion had been ready to give up. Ready to go down fighting the first time The Bitch gave him the opportunity. But her reluctance to come within his reach since then had instead given him the opportunity to reconsider.

The dream he'd woken from when she opened the door came back to him then in that muddled, fragmented way dreams are often recalled. But the memory of the real event it had been based on was much clearer.

Zion and the Trinity View Bisons had ultimately lost that game despite a spirited second half effort. It had indeed turned out to be the last time he put on the uniform. But when he left the field that night, he'd left it with his head held high, knowing he and his brothers gave everything they had. If nothing else, that's how he wanted to leave this life too.

24

You can fool yourself into believing almost anything if you try hard enough. Eventually, though, reality is going to come along and bash you in the head.

Charlotte had been fooling herself a lot lately. Fooling herself into believing she was a good person. Into believing that what she did, she did for the greater good. But how could it be true? Good people don't feed monsters.

Good people slay them.

Even allowing the thought to cross her mind—though it was not the first time—made Charlotte so dizzy she had to stop her jog and rest against the trunk of a tree. She pressed her palms against its rough bark and looked up through its leafy boughs to the cloudless, sun-soaked sky. She saw a bird, a hawk or a falcon, it looked like, gliding in circles on a current of warm air high above the ground. Somewhere deep in her soul, she wished she could trade places with it. But then this, too, brought a sinking feeling of despair; since when had making wishes ever done her any good? Even when they came true.

Especially when they came true.

With energy born from pent-up emotions still surging through her, Charlotte picked up her jog again. The trail she followed curled its way around the edge of her property, near where the fields met the forest. In the first few months following Malachi's birth, she had run it almost every day. Shedding the baby weight was what she'd told herself, and maybe she'd believed it back then. Looking back, Charlotte knew she'd run then for the same reason she ran now: because sometimes life gets too overwhelming to just stand still.

She couldn't be gone long, though. She tried to never stay gone for long, always hurrying to finish whatever errands had to be run. The anxiety she felt anytime she was away from the house had doubled ever since she started keeping prisoners in her basement.

Zion and his friends weren't the first. There'd been a swinger couple out of McKinney she'd kept down there for over a year. She'd sworn after them that she'd never keep captives again. Providing for Malachi's needs one meal at a time was easier, she'd decided, than trying to maintain a ready stock. Easier on her soul most of all; she didn't have to get to know the people she captured, didn't have to look at their pleading faces every day, when Malachi consumed them as soon as they were brought to him.

But this method of "just in time delivery" was also unreliable. And that made it risky. She had seen before what could happen when she took too long. Seen what Malachi swiftly became when the hunger was allowed to persist.

She slowed her pace again when she reached the part of the trail that ran parallel with the highway. Back in the early days, when her sister still visited the ranch, Lilibeth had expressed concerns about the safety of running on a trail within sight of an isolated rural highway. Someone driving by could spot her. And decide for all the wrong reasons to stop.

But now Charlotte almost wished it would happen. Wished someone else would do what she didn't have the courage to. Maybe this was the wish—the only wish—that would actually set things right.

A truck rolled by then. Old and dented and driving slow, exactly what you'd imagine an axe murderer would drive. Like a scene from a movie. Still jogging at a leisurely, unbothered pace, Charlotte pictured herself smiling as her murderer—her savior—got out of the pickup and strolled toward her, hatchet in hand. There would be pain, for a while, but then there'd be nothing. Right now, nothing sounded better than anything she could imagine.

But the pickup truck kept driving on. Charlotte watched its dusty tailgate disappear down the road. Probably some harmless farmer or ranch hand on their way back from a trip into town. If there was an axe or a rusty old chainsaw in the back of that truck, wood was surely all it had ever cut.

Only the good die young, Charlotte remembered. The ones like her—the wicked ones— tended to prosper in this upside-down world.

And my, she had prospered. The sight of her home, three stories of Colorado sandstone with panoramic windows and a covered porch, brought a flush of shame to her cheeks. Everyone wants what they don't have, and when you grow up impoverished, money seems like a one-way ticket to happiness. But Charlotte should have learned from all those frowning, miserable faces she used to serve and realized it would not make her happy either.

Had the rest been worth it at least? She wondered. She could have had a child no other way. It was Malachi—with all his unimaginable caveats—or nothing. And becoming the mother she'd never had herself was the one thing Charlotte had always wanted even more than the money.

Charlotte picked up her pace again and tried to let the exertion clear her thoughts. She wasn't sure why she put herself through this pointlessness so often. What's done was done. She'd made a deal with the devil. Signed her name in blood. And even if she had read the fine print—even if she had known—she knew deep down she would have done it anyway.

2 5

Stop, breathe, and think about what you're doing, Charlotte.

Glenda Robinson—Charlotte's favorite of all the foster parents she and Lilibeth had known in their younger years—used to tell her this all the time. But Charlotte rarely listened. She was a "leap before you look" kind of girl. Always had been. It was an easy thing to do, she'd found, when where you're leaping from was never where you wanted to be.

Except now more than any other time, maybe she needed to heed Mrs. Robinson's words. Going to meet a stranger who had just broken into her apartment was about as foolhardy as it gets. There was more than just the obvious danger, too. She could sense it clearly as she drove up the long, winding driveway that ended at a mansion on a hilltop. It made all the little hairs on the back of her arms stand rigid.

The gate at the entrance to the drive had been open when she arrived. As if the man who lived here was expecting her to come. Even though no sane woman would have. Maybe he knew she wasn't one of the sane ones, Charlotte thought. Maybe he already knew all about her.

There was only one way to find out. And that was the rub, really—if she hadn't come, if she'd just ignored the note or called the cops or done anything besides what he'd asked her to, she would never know the answer. Curious to a fault (and honestly not quite as attached to her life as most), Charlotte would've rather risked dying than live with the wondering.

It seemed like it took forever to reach the end of the drive. The road wound around the hill instead of going straight up it. And, without even meaning to, she'd been driving at a creeping pace.

Perfectly manicured hedges and lampposts bathing them in soft, white light passed by outside her windows. Up ahead, so high atop the hill she had to crane her neck to see it, the house glowed the same color, dozens of windows all alight. On the way here, she'd been picturing something much different. Something befitting the mystery of this man—a place Dracula would feel at home in—was what she'd imagined: pointed arches and flying buttresses, long, narrow windows without a light in sight. Instead, the house was bright and modern. The kind of place built by someone with good taste and the deepest of pockets.

She realized as she reached the end of the drive and her fingers touched the gearshift that this would be her last good chance to turn back. She could throw it into reverse instead of park. Hit the gas and squeal out of there, maybe even take out a hedge or two on the way as a middle finger to whomever lived here for entering her home uninvited.

Charlotte was good at daydreaming about doing the right thing. In her thoughts and intentions, she was always brave and virtuous. In reality, she was the kind of person who...well, who kept the bracelet. Who didn't call the police.

Who put the car in park and got out.

There was a fountain taller than most homes at the center of the bluestone roundabout—sculpted from gray marble into the form of three angels in a triangle with the tips of their outstretched wings touching. All three held urns in their hands, tipping them forward to let streams of water that shimmered in the moonlight cascade to the basin at their feet. Charlotte could smell the chlorine as she walked past it. For a moment, its steady, splashing churn drowned out all the worried voices in her head.

Walking up the marble steps to the home's entrance felt like walking the steps of the Capitol Building. Or the steps of some ancient temple—a wonder of the world in its time. There was a camera drilled into the marble archway above the towering double doors. Charlotte heard the soft hum of its motors and looked up just as it focused its black mirror eye on her. She saw a red light blinking beneath the lens and looked away, a little self-conscious. More than a little afraid.

She reached for the polished bronze knocker, but before her fingers touched it, she heard a latch retract. Then the door swung slowly open.

A man stood at the entrance, awash in a ribbon of golden light from a chandelier high above him. He was tall and slender, with a sharp jawline and bushy gray eyebrows. He wore a black tailcoat and white dress shirt beneath, perfectly pressed and starched. And though he made quite the distinguished impression, Charlotte knew this was not the man she was here to see. Men who owned a home like this one never answered their own door.

"Ms. Mallory," the butler said. And Charlotte felt a chill of creeping unease as she wondered how he knew her name. "Please, follow me."

Charlotte obeyed. As her heels clicked across the mirror polished floor, she found herself overwhelmed by the foyer's grandeur. A white marble staircase with ornate gold railing hugged the left wall and led to a balcony that circled the entire space. There were marble columns thick as tree trunks extending all the way to the high ceiling, and a chandelier with strings of crystals dangling down. Charlotte didn't recognize the art on the walls, but that wasn't saying much; no doubt each piece would've been just as at home in a fine museum. The place even smelled of luxury—sandalwood and leather and the cool, mineral scent of marble.

She followed the butler across the room and down a yawning hallway, then through a pair of double doors and into another hall that led to a sitting area. Here, there were a trio of black leather sofas positioned around a stone fireplace. Mounted above the hearth was a ram's head, its fur as polished and perfectly black as the furniture. Charlotte caught herself fixating on its yellow eyes—even knowing they were made of glass—before the butler spoke up and whisked her attention away.

"The master will be with you shortly," he said. And with that, he was gone. The room's walnut door clicked closed behind him.

The master? Charlotte felt like scoffing. But that's only what she pictured herself doing. In reality, the sound of it gave her chills.

She lowered herself onto the nearest sofa, slowly and carefully as if it were going to rip if she wasn't extra cautious; being in a room where every item likely cost more than a year of her wages only added to her paranoia.

She gazed up at the ceiling—so high even in this room that a fall from it would end in a splatter—and wondered how long she'd have to wait. It was her experience that the wealthy liked to keep people waiting. It sent a message, she supposed, that even their time was more valuable than yours.

But when she looked over her shoulder to scan the room only a few seconds later, Charlotte jumped a little in surprise. There was a man standing by the door. Somehow, he must have opened and closed it again without her hearing.

That or walked right through it, Charlotte thought, feeling cold all of a sudden as he stood there and stared at her.

His face was the first thing she noticed. It looked to have been chiseled from the same marble as his staircase, though his dark eyes and thin lips lent a sharp, predatory edge to his Greek statue aesthetic. His hair was dark, too, and long enough to touch his broad shoulders. When he lifted his arm to wave at her, it finally clicked. It was the same man she'd seen standing near Mrs. Allen's gate.

Charlotte started to stand—perhaps to greet him, perhaps to bolt out the door; she'd not yet made up her mind. But when he spoke to her, she stopped and listened.

"Hello, Charlotte. I'm pleased you accepted my invitation." His voice was low and hypnotic. It resonated in her ears in a way that brought goosebumps to the nape of her neck. And not necessarily the bad kind.

He strode across the room and sat down on the sofa adjacent to the one where she was seated. He propped a shoe so shiny black it reflected the light up on his knee and folded his hands across his lap. Charlotte watched him, at a loss for words and hoping he'd speak again. Hoping he'd start to unravel some of this mystery for her. But for a long while, he only watched her back.

"I came here..." Charlotte cleared her throat and started again. "I came here to find out what this was all about." She pulled her hand from her pocket and showed him the bracelet he'd left in her kitchen. But he never took his eyes off her, the glimmering diamonds seeming of no interest to him.

"I know why you came," he said. "And Mrs. Allen's bracelet is not the reason."

"Is this some kind of prank?"

"Do I look like a prankster to you?"

He most certainly didn't. Everything about the man—from his suit to his posture to his intense, coal-dark stare—exuded a deathly seriousness.

"I can't take this," Charlotte said.

The man sighed a little, that stare seeming to narrow on her even more. "I don't care what you do with the bracelet, Charlotte. Take it. Leave it. It's all the same to me."

"It's not mine to take. And it wasn't yours to give either."

"Oh, but it was. I purchased it fairly. Actually, it's funny how the worth of a thing varies from one person to another. Mrs. Allen would've told you that bracelet is worth $42,000 because that's what she paid for it, but she got taken for a ride on that one. Any jeweler worth their salt could tell you the clarity of those diamonds is subpar and would offer you ten, fifteen thousand for the

piece at most. And the gentleman I purchased it from...
well, it was only worth $500 and an eight ball of cocaine
to him.

"You see, Charlotte, I don't steal things," he continued.
"I make deals. And everything, everyone, has a price."

"So why give it to me then?" Charlotte asked.

"Consider it a down payment."

"For what?"

She saw him smile then for the first time, although it
was faint and never touched his cold, unblinking eyes.
"That's up to you. It all depends on what you want. And
how much you're willing to pay. So, tell me, Charlotte,
what is that you want?"

Charlotte started to smile herself. Whether he looked
the part of a trickster or not, surely this was indeed all a
joke. But then the feeling of a weight in her chest pressed
down and kept growing more intense. It seemed to pin
her to the sofa as the man's eyes continued to stare into
her soul, the magnitude of the moment so palpable it
was paralyzing. This was no prank, she realized. This was
something bigger than she could possibly comprehend.
Something with stakes so high they were dizzying. And
every nerve in her body could sense it.

"Go ahead," he said, his voice seeming to echo in her
ears. "Tell me what you want."

"I. . ." Charlotte swallowed and wondered somewhere
in the depths of her thoughts why speaking was suddenly

so difficult. Wondered why her words felt and sounded so drunken. "I want everything."

The man smiled again, but this time it was a wide and genuine grin. Dark flames seemed to dance in his eyes. Looking into those blazing eyes for long seemed like something that might drive a person insane. And yet she couldn't look away.

"That's the spirit, Charlotte," he cooed, the smooth rumble of his voice prickling her skin. "But you're going to have to be more specific than that, love."

Time slowed to a crawl. Charlotte closed her eyes. In the darkness, she could picture it so clearly. Everything her life was missing. Everything she'd never had and been told she never would. When she opened them again, she didn't even have to ask to know that the man—or whatever he was—had seen it all just as clearly.

"You write," he said.

Charlotte nodded.

"But you're not very good. Are you?"

Charlotte shook her head.

He leaned in, his voice an excited whisper. "Would you like to be? Would you like to be loved, Charlotte? Not by one or a few but by people all over the world. Would that make you happy?"

It would. Surely it would. But that's not all that she had pictured. There was something else she wanted just as badly. Something else she'd never had: a family.

"Say it, Charlotte. Tell me what else you desire," the man said. Him reading her thoughts didn't surprise her in the least. It seemed obvious almost. Entirely natural.

"It's not possible. The doctors told me—"

"They are merely men. And I am not bound by their limitations."

Charlotte believed him. Excitement and fear swirled through her in a disorienting mix.

"Say it," he reiterated. "You have to say it."

She considered for a moment. Considered all the possible implications, both those imaginable and those not. But was there even a price not worth paying for love? For the chance to love someone in the way she was never loved herself. For the chance to be loved back almost as much.

"I want to be a mother," she said.

She'd wanted it her whole life. But in a cruel twist of fortune, her ovaries had stopped functioning at the age of seventeen. Primary ovarian insufficiency is what the doctors had diagnosed her with. She could have adopted—it was not lost on her that doing so would be giving a child just like she used to be a mother and a home. But as an orphan herself, she also knew the reality: that some small yet irreplaceable part of the love she longed for was inherently biological.

"I can make that happen, Charlotte," the man said. "I can give you a child. I can give you wealth and fame and everything else you've ever dreamed of. All you have to do is accept my terms."

Yes. Charlotte was ready to say it—to shout it as loud as she could—already. But Mrs. Robinson's words came back to her again, and this time, for once, she listened. "What terms?" she asked.

"Think of them as truths, Charlotte," the man said. "Truths that are true of your world whether you accept them or not. Truth number one: all that is given can, and someday will, be taken away. Truth number two: every creature ever born must feed, consume, trample, and kill to survive. Morality is an illusion. One Nature can shatter at the drop of a hat."

Charlotte might not have understood what he was saying, but she was no less spellbound by every word. She didn't need to know their meaning to understand their magnitude. She could feel the weight of it like a ball and chain wrapped around her soul.

"What happens if I say no?" she asked.

"Nothing, Charlotte," the man said. "You'll leave here. Go back to your life. Back to surviving as best you can. And I will find another to accept my offer. I cannot see what your future will be if you say no. Only what it will be if you say yes."

With some effort, Charlotte closed her eyes. She couldn't take his gaze on her any longer, or the way it seemed to shrink the room and dim the lights so that all that existed were her and those dark, expectant eyes. But what she saw when she did frightened her even more: a picture of exactly what her life would be if she let this opportunity pass. All the loneliness and longing and regret. The regret most of all. How many times would she relive this moment if she said no, imagining the path not taken? Pleading for this miracle worker before her to return and give her one more chance.

"Yes," she said as she opened her eyes, spitting out the word before fear could stop her and ruin it all. "My answer is yes."

"Take my hand," the man said. She thought he'd be smiling, happy she'd accepted his offer, but his expression was colder than ever. And when she placed her hand in his, it, too, was as cold as stone.

Her vision swam. She would have fallen if he hadn't caught her. She could hear the garbled, distant sound of him speaking, but the words meant nothing to her. Just strange, hollow sounds from a world that was fading away.

It felt like sinking. Sinking into a trance she was quickly losing all desire to resist. Her feet seemed to float off the floor as he led her through the halls of his home. Waves of warmth rolled through her body, turning her muscles loose. With his arm around her waist, the man practically carried her up the marble stairs. But Charlotte didn't mind. Not in the slightest.

Time seemed to move like frames in a slideshow. One moment he was guiding her into a cavernous bedroom, firelight reflecting off the golden bedposts. The next moment he was undressing her, first her sweater and jeans, then her undergarments until everything she'd worn was lying on the hardwood floor. The next moment she was lying on the softest sheets her skin had ever touched. With him lying on top of her.

There was no pleasure in what came next. Not in the typical sense at least, and not for either one of them. His eyes were indeed full of lust as he took her, but it was clearly not for her. And though tears of joy sprang to her eyes before the act was even over, the act itself had nothing to do with them.

She could see it—painted across this stranger's coffered ceiling with the most vivid colors. Playing out like a movie on a projector screen, she watched the dreams she'd long given up on come to life.

The man on top of her finished silently, without a single twitch or grunt, as his piercing eyes continued to bore into hers. But Charlotte hardly noticed him anymore. The scenes unfolding on his ceiling had captured her full attention. Everything she'd ever wanted was painted there. Wealth, validation, acclaim, and, more than all of these, a child. One she could pour into all the love she'd never had the chance to share.

"I'll have Mr. Jefferies drive you home," the man said as he cinched up his trousers. "In your car, of course."

Charlotte started to say that wouldn't be necessary. But when she struggled to even form the words, she realized that maybe it was. Colors still danced on the ceiling above her, but they were starting to fade. The warm, fuzzy feeling that had enveloped her from scalp to toe tips was fading too, and the draft felt suddenly cold against her bare skin. On unsteady legs, Charlotte stood, gathered her clothing from the floor, and began to dress.

The man held the bedroom door for her—a polite gesture on the surface, but the impatience resting beneath his stone expression was not difficult to spot. Charlotte got the feeling he had no desire to hide it.

"Will I see you again?" she asked as he gestured down the hall, pointing out the direction she should go—and sooner rather than later, it felt.

"Not for a while."

Charlotte started to leave but risked one last question. "I never got your name?"

"Because I never offered it," he said. "Go home now, Charlotte. Our business has concluded for now."

Charlotte knew better than to argue. Like a mouse knows better than to argue if a cat lets it free. And suddenly, that's just what it felt like. Fight or flight instincts (just flight actually. Who was she kidding?) surged through her muscles as the daze she'd been in just moments before melted away like morning frost.

Her heels clacked against the marble as she practically sprinted down the hall. It would have been embarrassing under any other circumstance, running from a man's bedroom like a jilted one-night stand, but something told her that's exactly what he expected her to do.

The butler, Mr. Jefferies, was waiting for her in the foyer. He reached out his palm, presumably for her keys, but Charlotte brushed right past him. She hurried to her car and drove away as fast as she dared down the steep, winding drive.

Three weeks later, after learning she was pregnant, she did try to return. When her phone's GPS app refused to recognize the address (despite pulling it up with no issue the first time), Charlotte ignored the twisting feeling in her stomach and attempted to find the way by memory. When the sun set and an entire day of driving around the upscale neighborhoods of Preston Hollow yielded no sign of that mansion on a hill, she could take the bewilderment no more. She drove home and swore to try and never think of the man whose child she carried ever again.

26

A needle-prick pain in Manuel's left earlobe rose to a piercing intensity. It was a mosquito, no doubt—a big fat one by the feel of it. There were plenty of them to be found swarming the swampy banks of Lake Kinley. But the sheriff was too distracted to even slap it away.

His eyes were fixed on the spot in the green water where two thick chains disappeared below the surface. Next to him, the winch of a tow truck groaned and whined, pulling the tense, popping chain along one slow twist at a time.

Bubbles rose from the silty lake bottom, some forty feet down according to the dive team. A few seconds later, Manuel saw the four lift bags those divers had attached to the vehicle breach the surface, then a dark shadow just beneath them, rising from the depths one chain link at a time.

He knew even before the vehicle's front bumper broke the surface exactly whose car it would be. Manuel had never put much stock in psychics or ESP, but he did believe it was possible for a person to just know things sometimes. Stephen King, in one of the few books Manuel had ever read for pleasure, called it "the shine," and he had believed there to be a grain of truth to that part of the story.

The farther the vehicle surfaced, the more it proved his intuition. It was silver. And a sedan. And even from across the water, he could see the blue and white BMW emblem on its mesh grill. It would take checking the plate to know for certain, but Manuel was already sure.

He reached for the radio on his vest and started to turn the knob to the channel that would connect him to state dispatchers. He'd need them to send down a forensics team. For all the good it would do; divers had already confirmed there weren't any bodies in the vehicle, and seven months at the bottom of Lake Kinley was bound to have destroyed any other DNA evidence.

But just as he was about to turn the radio from its primary channel, a voice cut through the speaker.

"Sheriff? You copy?"

It was Deputy Hale. She had gone on the boat with the dive team. Manuel could see her standing near its bow, her radio in hand.

"What is it?" he said, squeezing and releasing the radio's push-to-talk button.

"We've got another vehicle on the sonar. About twenty feet north of where the other one was."

"No shit?" Manuel said. This was the last thing he expected.

"No shit."

Manuel's mind began to race. Multiple vehicles meant multiple victims. This wasn't a one-off incident they'd discovered.

It was a dumping ground. A dumping ground for a serial killer.

"We need more boats," he said. And definitely a forensics unit now. Hell, maybe even the FBI. Part of him wanted to keep the case for himself. He could already envision his county crawling with feds, and he and his deputies relegated to the sidelines in their own backyard. But they'd be in over their heads with something like this. Most of the cops in Wayne County—of which there were not many—had never even worked a cut-and-dry homicide case before. Folks in these parts were just too few and too friendly to kill each other all that often.

"See if you can get them to send ones with a better sonar system on them," Deputy Hale said. "It's gonna take a lot of time to search the rest of the lake."

Manuel hadn't thought of this yet. He didn't know much about the sonar on the one boat Wayne County Sheriff's Department owned, but Lake Kinley covered almost sixty acres. It would take days to search it even with the staties helping. And no telling what they'd find.

"I'll get the calvary on the way," he said.

"Roger that."

By the time Manuel finished explaining the situation to the dispatcher at Texas DPS, the tow truck had pulled the silver BMW all the way to the bank. Manuel trudged through the cattails and water-sogged soil to get a look at its plate.

There was algae covering a couple of the numbers, but the rest matched up and confirmed what he already knew in his gut. The car belonged to Clint Davis. All four of its windows were rolled down—another strong sign it was sunken intentionally. And when Manuel peered inside, he saw the most certain evidence yet: a slime-covered cinderblock lodged against the accelerator.

"You alright, Sheriff?" asked the tow truck driver, a lean and wiry old man by the name of Leroy Moore. By this point, everyone in the area knew about Sheriff Garcia's nephew and the vehicle he'd gone missing in. Especially a man as plugged into the barbershop chatter as Leroy was.

"Yeah," Manuel said. It didn't matter whether it was true or not. All his thoughts of Zion and Marissa and how she would take this news would have to wait for now. "Why don't you go ahead and pull this a little farther up onto the bank. There's a lot needs to be done before we can take it out of here. Actually, you might as well unhook and go on home after. No telling how long it's gonna take."

"I'll stick around. If that's alright. Won't charge any extra for it either."

Manuel could tell he really wanted to. There wasn't a lot of excitement left for a man his age in this tame and humdrum pocket of the world.

"That's fine. Just pull it up a little farther so the state boys don't have to get their shiny boots all muddy."

"Yessir."

By four o'clock in the afternoon, there were five boats trolling the waters of Lake Kinley and twice as many state vans, trucks, and cruisers parked along the bank. People driving down Highway 43 would predictably slow to a crawl as they passed the short lake access road. One look was all it required to know something serious—something *interesting*—was going on.

And it kept getting more and more interesting, too. They'd found three more vehicles in addition to the two they'd already discovered. Dive teams had been in and out of the water all day, attaching chains and lift balloons. Checking for bodies. So far, all the vehicles had been empty.

The state police intended to sweep the entirety of Lake Kinley with sonar before the day was done, and Manuel figured from watching the boats they'd covered about half of it so far. He also figured they were unlikely to find anything else.

All five of the vehicles they'd pulled up so far had been within a hundred yards of each other—all a straight shot from a bend in the access road near the steepest part of the bank where a person could line a car up, jam the accelerator, and count on it not only making it to the water but sinking a long way down when it did.

Texas DPS must have arrived at the same theory; crime scene investigators had been crawling that bank for the past two hours, taking photos and examining the ground for tracks. There were even more of them bustling around the rusted, algae-covered vehicles lined up along the bank. Manuel sat on the hood of his cruiser and watched them work. At this point, there wasn't much else for him to do.

Eventually, a man from their number wearing blue jeans and a black cowboy hat approached. He extended a gloved hand, and Manuel shook it.

"Sheriff. My name's Detective Steve Wilson. Was wondering if you might help me clear a couple things up."

"I'll do what I can."

"First off…" Detective Wilson stopped and slapped his neck hard. He examined the splotch of blood and mosquito guts on his palm before continuing. "First off, how did you come to find out about the first vehicle? The one you boys had pulled up before we got here."

"A magnet fisherman called it in," Manuel said.

"Come again?"

"A magnet fisherman. They put magnets on the end of a line and troll lakes and riverbeds. Looking for stuff people drop, I assume. Except this one pulled up a muffler."

"I see. And that vehicle was the one your nephew and those two other boys out of Dallas went missing in, is that right?"

"That's right."

Detective Wilson sniffed. "Well, we've run the VINs on four of the five vehicles, counting the BMW. They're all connected to missing persons cases too. There's a Chevy Trailblazer that's too corroded for us to get a VIN or a plate number right now. If we get it into a lab, they might be able to work some magic there. Either way, I'd bet my next paycheck it's the same story with that one."

"Who are the other missing persons?"

"Old Vietnam vet out of Grand Prairie, went missing two years ago. Then there's a middle-aged couple from Las Vegas last seen four years ago in McKinney. The one we just pulled out is the one I actually want to talk to you about. It belonged to a girl named Becka Green. You recognize that name?"

Manuel did. It was the lesbian girl from Hooper Lake who'd gone missing two years ago. Last seen at The Sapphire Lounge. "Yeah. I know who she is."

"I'd like to have a look at those case files. If Quantico doesn't swoop in before then, that is. I don't need to tell you that this is a big deal, Sheriff. It's the kind of thing that's likely to get national attention soon as word gets out."

Manuel sighed. The detective was indeed not telling him anything he didn't already know, and he dreaded the shitshow to come. Reporters and special agents crawling all over his county would only be the half of it. When folks found out there was a murderer on the loose, there was bound to be a lot of fear and tension. Pressure on his department, DPS, and anyone else involved to solve the case and make the streets safe again would be immense.

Of course, they wouldn't exactly be *told* there was a murderer on the loose. There hadn't been a single body found yet, after all. But anyone with any kind of sense would reach the same conclusion every cop on the scene had already reached: that whoever sunk those five cars in Lake Kinley had almost certainly killed their occupants.

"With your permission, Sheriff," Detective Wilson said, "I'd like to have these vehicles taken to the state crime lab in Garland."

"Go ahead," Manuel said. He didn't have any real grounds to protest. The Garland geeks—as he somewhat lovingly called the forensic scientists working at what was the nearest state crime lab—would be much better equipped to analyze the vehicles than his department.

"We need to catch the sonofabitch who did this ASAP. This is the kind of thing that'll make or break a person's career."

Manuel, who had climbed the political ladder as far as he intended to and was now nearing retirement, no longer cared about such things. But he did care about catching the son of a bitch.

"I'm thinking about giving the feds a call," Manuel said. He watched Detective Wilson's caterpillar eyebrows drop. Now he was the one faced with having the case snatched away from him.

"Let's work it ourselves a while, Sheriff. That's my opinion, anyhow. I'm sure you know how much getting them involved can…*complicate* things sometimes."

He did, and it could. But the FBI could also bring special expertise to bear. Criminal profilers and behavioral analysts who could study the victims and spot patterns that would shed light on their abductor. Forensics experts much more equipped and qualified than even those at Garland.

"I'll hold off for a while, Detective," Manuel said. "But not very long. I'm too old and too tired to care about anything but getting this guy behind bars. Otherwise, you wouldn't be here either."

Detective Wilson nodded. "Understood." But the new resolve in his eyes told the whole story. He was young, with plenty of ambition and hunger in his belly, and he wanted this one bad.

Manuel did too, for different reasons. He caught himself staring at the corpse of the BMW that Zion, surely a corpse himself now, had gone missing in. Someone had killed that boy, and a whole lot of others too by the looks of it. And they'd been doing it for a while. Right under his nose.

Watching Detective Wilson return to the forensics team still working the vehicles, Manuel made a decision sure to disappoint him; he was going to call Quantico as soon as he got back to the office.

27

The crack and grind of the brush hog's spinning blades striking a rock made Charlotte wince. The last thing she needed was to tear something up and have to spend the whole day fixing it. It was likely to take several more hours to get the entire place mowed as it was.

Not that it even needed to be mowed that badly. She'd come out here to distract herself as much as anything. To get away from the news. Every channel she'd flipped to was covering the same story. Not just the local ones, but the national ones too. CNN, ABC, the whole lot of them.

Of course, she'd known about the vehicles in Lake Kinley being found well before they started talking about it on TV. Word spreads like wildfire in a small town, and the influx of cops and media vans would've been hard to miss.

It was a chilling thought, picturing all the agents and officers who were scrutinizing every inch of those five cars right this moment. She'd been careful not to leave any evidence in them, and she hoped that all that time in the water would have destroyed anything like hair or fingerprints.

She hoped but wasn't sure.

What would happen if they caught her? Her fate would be obvious—three hots and a cot for the rest of her days—but Malachi's fate was much more nebulous. She could only imagine what they'd do to him if they discovered what he was—what kind of black site abyss they'd keep him in, what kind of tests and experiments they'd run the rest of his life. And if not that, it would be what *he* did to *them.*

Death was better, she decided. Better for both of them. If it came down to it, that's what she'd do. Or at least that's what she'd try and do. Charlotte didn't know for sure if she was capable of it. In more ways than one.

For the next three hours, she drove her tractor in circles beneath the searing July sun. The place looked nice by the end, but Charlotte certainly didn't. Her tank top was soaked through with sweat, and her arms and neck were burned cherry-red despite the generous glob of sunscreen she'd applied.

What she wanted to do was shower and take a nice long nap. Maybe sleep all the way through to next morning. What she had to do instead was fix dinner and clean out Zion's waste bucket.

First, a shower, though. That part was non-negotiable. Once she'd parked the tractor in the barn and walked back to the house, the air conditioner's chill gave her a welcome greeting at the door. She stopped in the kitchen for a glass of ice water, then headed upstairs.

She stopped again outside Malachi's bedroom door and listened for him inside. But all she could hear was the whoosh of his ceiling fan.

"Malachi? You in there?"

"Yeah," he immediately replied. A hint of relief washed away the hint of dread that creeps in a hundred times a day for all parents, but especially for her.

"Whatcha doing?"

"Reading."

Charlotte both liked and disliked this. Books offered an escape from the dull, isolated life Malachi was forced to live. But in doing so, they also kindled longings that could never be fulfilled. Regardless, she'd decided when he first began to show interest in books that she wasn't going to deny him this as well.

"I'm gonna take a shower, then you can help with dinner, alright?"

"Alright, Momma."

Charlotte started to open the door, just to see him, but decided to leave him to his book. She stripped out of her clothing in her bedroom, tossing the sweaty garments into the hamper by the closet, then stepped into the attached master bathroom.

The shower was one she'd had custom-installed, right after *Torched Hearts* hit the shelves and made her more money than she could spend in the next thirty years. It had a frameless glass enclosure, granite floors, and a bronze showerhead with settings she still hadn't mastered. Charlotte had been pretty proud of it at one point in time.

Normally, she preferred her showers bordering on scalding, but not after a long day in the heat. She turned the water to somewhere between lukewarm and frigid and drew in a sharp breath as it washed over her feverish skin.

Charlotte closed her eyes and let her head go blank. Whatever the reason, the shower had always been the only place she was capable of truly clearing her thoughts. She could meditate like a monk as long as there was water streaming down her face and gurgling in her ears. For this reason, she always tended to take long showers. Especially lately.

She couldn't have said how long this one was, but the tips of her fingers had all turned to prunes by the time she finally shut the water off. She dried off and put on fresh clothes, then stepped into the hallway and knocked on Malachi's door.

"Hey, kiddo. You ready to come help with dinner?"

No answer. Charlotte turned the knob and opened the door.

She expected to see him on his bed, eyes closed and mouth drooped open with a book across his chest. She'd found him this way plenty of times before. But the room was empty.

Another twinge of that ever-present dread pricked her heart. It was needless worry, though. Malachi might have been confined to the ranch, but he wasn't confined to his bedroom. Even on days as hot as this one, he liked to play outside.

She headed downstairs and opened the front door. A blast of hot air that didn't feel so bad after the cold shower rushed in to greet her. Charlotte scanned the front yard. Then the field beyond it. Then the gravel road leading to the stables. But she saw no sign of her son.

"Malachi!"

Nothing. Now the dread was stronger—and not so unreasonable anymore. Malachi rarely strayed far. And he always answered when called.

The stable was the first logical place to look. Malachi liked hanging out with the horses sometimes, though if he was in there, or anywhere nearby at all, he would have surely heard her. It was worth checking anyway, she decided.

Instead, on instinct or impulse, Charlotte turned back inside. She couldn't see the door to the basement from where she stood, but it called to her. Called to her in a way that made her stomach flip.

When she rounded the corner and saw it there in the shadows of the hallway, the deadbolt was the first thing she noticed. The thumb turn was facing the wrong direction, pointing left toward the door's center instead of right toward its reinforced frame.

The door's second lock—the one that required a key to open even from the outside—gave no such indication as to whether it was still secured. But Charlotte already assumed the worst. Her mind raced as she tried to remember where she'd left the key.

Then it hit her. It had been in the front pocket of her jeans. The ones she'd tossed into the hamper without even thinking about it and left unsupervised for however long her lengthy shower had been.

Charlotte tried the knob and felt her heart drop when it did exactly what she dreaded: turn without catching. She pushed open the door and started down the stairs, already bracing for the carnage she was sure to find.

2 8

When the basement door creaked open and a ribbon of light spilled down the stairs, Zion paid it no attention. Today (tonight? Damned if he knew in this clockless, windowless room) had not been a good one. And that was saying something considering the standard for good and bad days at this point in his life.

First, it had been the headache he woke up with. Then the hopelessness that wasn't anything new but hit so much harder some days than others. He'd tried to read for a while, then tried watching *Jurassic Park* for the billionth time; The Bitch's supply of books was a lot more exhaustive than her supply of DVDs for the flatscreen she'd moved down. For the past few hours, he'd just been lying on the couch, waiting until he was sleepy enough to pass the time unconscious. That was by far the most pleasant way to pass it anymore.

What he probably should be doing was capitalizing on every opportunity The Bitch gave him to win her over. This time, though, he figured he'd just lie there with his eyes closed while she did whatever she came to do. Maybe it might win him a few sympathy points anyway if she saw him there, too dejected to even look up at her.

But then he heard the footsteps coming down the stairs. They weren't normal. They weren't *hers*. Jolting all the way awake in an instant, Zion leapt off the couch and turned around.

He was right. It wasn't The Bitch who had opened the door. Halfway down the stairs already was the boy Zion had seen three weeks ago. The freakishly tall one. And freakish in more ways than just that. His pulse began to climb, but Zion kept a straight face.

The boy stared at him for a beat longer, then bounded the rest of the way down the stairs. For a moment, Zion had the feeling he was charging him, and his muscles tensed. But the boy slowed down once he reached the last step and strolled nonchalantly past the perimeter of Zion's chain.

"Hey," the boy said.

"Hey," Zion said back,

"My mom doesn't know I'm down here." Such a thin voice coming from such a large body set Zion's hairs even more on end.

"Okay."

"She's probably gonna be mad. At me, not at you."

"What are..." Zion cleared his throat and started again. Something about the way the boy's dark eyes bore into him made speaking difficult. "What are you doing down here then?"

The boy shrugged. "I dunno."

"Sooo..."

"You like watching movies?"

"Yeah," Zion said. "I think most people do."

"What's your favorite?"

"My what?"

"Your favorite movie."

"Um…*Jurassic Park*." That was a lie. *Anchorman* would have been the real answer, but he doubted the kid had ever seen it.

The boy's eyes lit up then, though not in a way that set Zion at ease any. "I *love* that movie! You remember when the T-rex gets that one guy while he's sitting on the toilet? Then he was all like…" The boy snapped at the air hard enough for Zion to hear the clack of his teeth, then he shook his head side to side to imitate the way the T-rex had thrashed Donald Gennaro's body in the movie before swallowing him down.

"Uh-huh."

The boy jerked his head one more time to get the disheveled curls of black hair out of his eyes, then said, "My name's Malachi. What's yours?"

"Zion."

Malachi grinned, then burst out singing. "*We're marching to Zion, beautiful, beautiful Zion.* Like that one?"

"Yeah…I guess," Zion said. "That's a church hymn, right? That song."

"What's a churchhim?"

"Never mind."

"Mom just sings to me sometimes. I know *Sweet Caroline* too. Wanna hear that one?"

"Umm—"

"Actually, let's do something else."

"Like what?" Zion asked.

Before answering, Malachi plopped down on the couch beside him. "Is that my Xbox?" he asked, pointing to the console sitting beneath the TV on the plastic stand's sole shelf.

"Is it?"

"Yeah, but it's alright. Mom bought me a new one for my birthday last year. Hey, did she bring Minecraft down here too?"

"Yeah," Zion said. It made sense now why all the games had been E-rated.

"Wanna play?"

He really didn't. He wanted this interaction to be over—with every fiber of his creeped-out being—but Zion was starting to sense an opportunity. If this kid belonged to The Bitch, winning his favor would be a whole lot easier than winning hers. And maybe even more valuable.

"Sure," he said. "I'm down."

Malachi's face lit up again. "I gotta show you the castle I built. It's got a moat and everything. Wait, you didn't delete my saved worlds, did you?"

Zion shook his head, even though he really couldn't remember. He hoped he hadn't. Malachi fetched the Xbox controller from the TV stand and turned it on.

He had not, in fact, deleted the saves, Zion learned a few moments later. And Malachi was giddy to show him all the builds he'd constructed in yesteryears before the arrival of his new console.

Zion, with as much enthusiasm as he could muster, oohed and aahed over each one. It was way over the top, and any adult with an ounce of social savvy would have sniffed it out as patronizing. But Zion noticed the more excited he acted, the more excited Malachi became too.

By the time his enthusiasm for the game finally began to wane, Zion guessed they'd been at it for almost half an hour. Malachi had shown him about all there was to show, and Zion was eager to make the most of however much time remained before The Bitch came storming down the stairs.

"So how come your mom doesn't let you come down here?" Zion asked. "We could do this all the time, you know."

Malachi frowned a little, the grin on his face subsiding for the first time since they powered up the Xbox. "Yeah…wish we could. I don't really have any friends. Except for Mom."

"So why can't we?"

"I dunno," Malachi said. It seemed to be his favorite phrase. But this time, Zion could tell he *did* know. The way his cheeks blushed and his eyes dropped to his bare feet revealed the truth.

"I just don't see what the big deal is really," Zion said. "Like, I'm down here all by myself all the time. And you just said you don't have anyone to play with either. What's your mom afraid of?"

The way the boy looked at him then, it was all Zion could do not to slide away from him a little farther down the couch. A coldness seemed to settle over his features. Now more than ever, he looked much older than his rounded face and spotless skin would suggest.

"I don't think she wants us to be friends," he said.

"Why would…why not?"

Malachi leaned in a little closer. Close enough for the sickly sweet scent of his prepubescent sweat to fill the air. His eyes narrowed and fixed Zion in place like a pushpin through the back of a butterfly. Zion tried to swallow but nearly choked on his own spit when the muscles in his throat declined to cooperate.

Because you're not going to be around much longer.

Zion heard the words not in his ears but inside his head. Like an inner thought spoken in someone else's voice. A wave of vertigo hit him, and it felt like he was going to be sick.

Just then, the basement door flung open. Malachi jerked his eyes away, and Zion almost collapsed. He took a gasping breath, then looked up to see The Bitch bounding down the stairs.

"Malachi! What on earth are you doing?"

Malachi shot Zion a sheepish half grin. A "we're busted" grin just like the ones Zion and his friends used to share when they were kids and their parents caught them red-handed. Like he was just an ordinary kid himself and not some towering freak capable of...whatever *the fuck* that had been.

"Nothing, Momma. Just playing video games."

"Get up here!" his mother demanded. "Right now." Malachi slumped his shoulders and obeyed. He dragged his feet across the floor with each step, making a *swoosh-swoosh* sound against the cement. "Hurry up!"

She grabbed him so swiftly as soon as he was within her reach that Zion thought she was about to try and lift him over her shoulder. All five foot nothing of her and six foot plus of him. But instead, she just held him firmly by the arm and hurried him back up the stairs.

She took one look back at Zion before she left. Just long enough for him to see a crack in the mask of indifference she wore so diligently—and spot a glimpse of the sheer terror beneath it.

29

BEFORE

Charlotte screamed. She screamed so loud it hurt her throat. Not that she noticed. That pain was like a matchstick in the center of the sun compared to the cramping, ripping pressure in her abdomen.

It came in waves, and she dreaded the start of each one. This one lasted so long it felt she might pass out from holding her breath. When the room with its white floor and white walls and nurses in scrubs all gathered around her bed started to swim, Charlotte clenched her eyes shut and begged for it to end.

"Keep breathing, honey," one of the nurses—one of the *male* nurses said. As if breathing was still easy as ever when it felt like your insides were being crushed in a vice.

She didn't know what—no one had told her—but something was wrong. The pain, the blood, the doctors' hushed conversations were all easy-to-read signs even in her state. Finally, one of them knelt next to her and spelled it out.

"Charlotte, you're doing so well, but listen to me, okay?" she said.

Between her mask and cap and thick-lensed glasses, Charlotte couldn't say what the woman looked like, but her voice sounded warm. Serious, but warm. Charlotte nodded, hoping she'd get out whatever she had to say before the next wave crashed.

"The placenta has separated prematurely. It's called a placental abruption, and I've seen it plenty of times before. You and the baby are both going to be alright. But I need you to stay strong for me. We've got to make sure this doesn't cause fetal distress. And that means we're not going to be able to give you an epidural."

Charlotte couldn't stop the sobs from spilling. The epidural—hoping that any minute she might be far enough along for them to give it to her—had been the only thing keeping her sane. Now that it was snatched away, she stared at the pool of blood soaking into the sheets and wondered how much more she would have to lose before death took the pain away.

For the next six hours, though, there was no such release. She screamed until her vocal cords were too strained to keep going. She cried until her tear ducts ran dry. And every time the pain reached its pinnacle, she thought it would surely kill her. Thought no human could possibly endure such torment and keep on living. The fact she did—the fact her body would ever allow such agony—felt like a terrible betrayal.

Then it happened. One last nauseating, excruciating push, and the pain subsided. She sucked in a breath. And for the first time in his life, so did her baby boy. Charlotte closed her eyes and listened to him cry while the nurses tended to him. It sounded beautiful and heartbreaking and terrifying all in one.

It was a while before she got to hold him. There was bleeding to stop first. Tears to suture. Now that her body was hers alone again, the doctors offered nitrous oxide in addition to the local anesthetic they'd injected, but Charlotte refused. She'd made it this far without any drugs. No reason to be foggy-headed now, when she was about to hold her son for the very first time.

The doctors worked quickly. It probably didn't even take them that long, but it felt like ages. Her baby had stopped crying and seemed to be sleeping now. Charlotte watched the nurse holding him against her shoulder with burning impatience and envy.

"Are you ready to hold him now, Momma?" the nurse asked. Charlotte had never heard a question so unnecessary. When the nurse placed him against her bare chest, his skin on hers, she felt a warmth rush through her like none she had ever felt before.

His hair, of which he already had nearly a full head of, was raven black. His skin, though reddened by increased circulation, was already darker than hers before the first ray of sunlight ever touched it. When his eyelids drows-ily opened and his eyes lifted to see her face, Charlotte swore she could actually feel her heart expanding to make room for all the love.

"Have you decided on a name for him yet?" the nurse asked, clipboard now in hand.

Charlotte had. She was going to name him after his great-grandfather, Malachi Humphrey. She had never met the man, he'd died before Charlotte was ever born, but it was a good name. And, from what little she'd heard others speak of him, he was a good person.

"His name is..."

Charlotte trailed off. There was someone standing near the corner of the room. Not a doctor or a nurse, though a nurse did walk right past him without even a glance in his direction. He watched Charlotte with dark yet fiery eyes she would have recognized even apart from his sculpted face and ten-thousand-dollar suit.

His name is Abaddon.

The man's mouth never moved as he spoke, and no one else in the room seemed to hear him. But Charlotte heard him clear as crystal—chilling as an arctic grave.

That's what you will call him.

"Charlotte," the nurse said. "Are you alright?"

Charlotte blinked a couple of times, but the man in the corner of the room was still there. She tore her eyes away from him and focused on the nurse.

"I'm alright."

The nurse gave her a soft smile. "Do you have a name for him, dear?"

Abaddon

"Yes," Charlotte said. "His name is Malachi. Malachi James Mallory."

"It's a good name," the nurse said once she'd written it down, patting Charlotte's arm.

His father must not have thought so. Even though she avoided looking where he stood, Charlotte could feel his gaze searing into her soul. Shadows seemed to fill the room, swirling up from the ground and down from the ceiling, expanding from the dark corners of the room until the entire space was just as dark. Until the only light that remained was a pair of eyes like flaming furnaces in the corner of the room.

I will not be denied, Charlotte.

Deep in her heart, she knew it was true. Eventually, this man...this thing...would claim what he was owed. There was nothing anyone in the world could do to stop it.

But, for now, the boy was hers. And, for now, his name was Malachi.

30

"What did he tell you?" Charlotte asked, cutting straight to the chase. No point in beating around the bush when she held a 9mm in her hand; that already set a pretty serious tone.

Zion looked down at the gun, then back up at her. Charlotte narrowed her eyes and raised it so he could see it from an angle most people hope to never see a firearm. So he could see that perfect, pitch-dark little circle looking back at him.

Of course, the gun was just a clump of steel and polymer without any bullets, and Charlotte had never even opened the box of ammunition she'd purchased along with it. But even if he guessed that, she doubted he'd bet his life on it.

"Whoa. Just…calm down. I swear he didn't tell me anything."

"Nothing? Down here all that time and he didn't speak a word?"

"Well yeah, I mean, he talked. He showed me his games. We talked about movies."

"What else?"

Zion, who'd had his hands up ever since she raised the gun, let them drop a little. "Can you please stop pointing it at me? It's not my fault he came down here. I'll tell you whatever you want to know."

Charlotte considered it for a moment, then lowered the gun. The way Zion visibly relaxed made her think it might have been the wrong move. Or was it better if he was relaxed? She really didn't have a clue. Didn't have any idea what she was doing. Not in this moment or at any point in the last seven and a half years.

"He just wanted to hang out," Zion said. "I didn't know what to do."

Charlotte studied him. She was no expert interrogator—that much was obvious—but her judgement was he told the truth. "I'm not mad at you."

To her surprise, Zion laughed out loud at this. The kind of nervous, uncontrollable burst born of pent-up emotion and as close to sobs as real laughter. "Do you always point guns at people you aren't mad at?"

Charlotte blushed and hated herself for it. She slipped the 9mm into the pocket of her shorts, wondering why she'd even brought it. She thought about what he'd said, and before she could help it, she laughed herself. Probably for the same reasons he had.

"I'm sorry," she said, wiping at tears. "I don't know what got into me."

"It's all good," Zion said. "It's actually not the first time I've had a gun pointed at me."

"Were you in a gang?" Charlotte asked.

"No..." Zion said. She realized a moment too late how racist that sounded and felt yet another needle of guilt stab her pincushion soul. "My cousin found his dad's pistol back when we were little kids and pointed it at my head. Uncle Trey whipped him with a belt for it when he found out. Even though it was his fault for leaving the gun out."

"Oh. I'm sorry that I thought…"

"Don't worry about it."

"I want you to know something," Charlotte said after a long moment's silence. Then she went silent again. Where was she going with this? She had no idea, but she needed to say it anyway.

"Know what?"

Charlotte sighed. "Look, I know it doesn't mean shit, but I am sorry."

"About the gang thing or…"

"No, about…all of this. Keeping you here. What happened to your friends."

"And what's that, Charlotte?" His eyes and voice both dripped with sudden emotion—fear and pleading and anger all mixed together. "What happened to my friends?"

This was why bringing it up had been a mistake. She should have seen it coming. "Never mind. Forget I mentioned it."

Zion shook his head. "Nah…Nah, see, I can't just forget about it. Not when I'm down here by myself every day and that's all I ever think about."

"The truth would not make it any easier," Charlotte said. "Trust me."

"Maybe. Maybe not. But what difference is it to you?"

It was a fair question. Honestly, it didn't matter what she told him. In fact, she realized something then: Zion was the only person in the world she actually *could* tell the truth to. She could tell him anything she wanted—talk about whatever she wanted—with no repercussion. He was quite literally a captive audience. And soon enough, whatever she shared would die with him.

She'd been so adamant about keeping the truth from him, but for what reason? Suddenly, she couldn't say.

Charlotte closed her eyes for a beat, then opened them to see Zion still staring at her expectantly. She sighed sharply and shook her head, entirely unsure of what she was about to do. "You're not going to believe it even if I do tell you. You're just gonna think I'm crazy."

"No offense," Zion said, with maybe just a touch of humor in his expression. "I kind of already do."

Charlotte laughed again, another burst of emotion she had no hope of containing. Then she sat down and told him everything.

31

The Bitch was crazy. That was the only possible explanation. It had been all Zion could do to sit there and listen to her ravings, nodding his head and pretending to believe. Faking the appropriate shock and fear would have been impossible for him, but he didn't actually have to fake that part. It was genuinely shocking just how far gone she really was. And genuinely terrifying too.

He was relieved when she finally left. He immediately put a movie on the TV—*Iron Man*, just because it was the first one he grabbed off the shelf—and tried to put everything she told him from his mind. Because as much as it frightened him knowing he was held captive by someone completely detached from reality, the possibility she told the truth frightened him even more.

Something was wrong with that kid. Malachi. That much was definitely true. What he'd done—the way he'd spoken without words—was the one thing about their interaction that Zion had kept from The Bitch. Mostly because he had no idea what to make of it himself. Then there was the size of him, of course. And how creepy he acted. And the way Clint had just followed him up the stairs like a lost puppy when he could have easily run.

But no. It still couldn't be what she'd said. It wasn't possible. And the more he thought about it, the crazier he was going to make himself. Probably end up as crazy as her if he didn't get a grip.

So, he tried to keep his breathing steady and tried to focus on the movie. It was at the part where Tony Stark is stuck in the cave, working on building his first suit out of spare parts. In the movies, the good guys always figured out how to escape. In the real world, it wasn't so easy.

Except there had been one other thing The Bitch had told him. The one part he actually hoped was true. Apparently, the cops had found Clint's BMW. And not just his car, but a whole bunch of others too.

He wasn't sure why she'd told him this; maybe once she started talking, the floodgates just burst open. Or maybe that part was bullshit too. At least that story made sense, though. Because surely the police were looking for him. Surely someone as insane as her couldn't have covered her tracks that perfectly.

Lying on the couch, Zion closed his eyes and imagined what it would be like to see an army of police officers storming down the stairs, perhaps with Uncle Manuel leading the charge. He normally tried to steer clear of law enforcement as much as possible. But cops were like seat belts and bike helmets: annoying until you need them to save your life.

Was Uncle Manuel out there right now, turning the whole state upside down looking for him? It heartened Zion to think so. But, then again, it'd been years since they'd even spoken. He could hardly picture what his uncle looked like anymore. Zion's mom had never forgiven Uncle Manuel for the drinking, and what happened to his grandfather as a result of it. Maybe he had every right not to really care that Zion was missing.

But then Zion remembered something his uncle had told him when he was just a little kid. Something about family being the only thing that matters in this world. And he remembered, too, how much he seemed to have meant it.

Even as defeated as he felt, Zion was certain Uncle Manuel would turn over every stone in Texas to find him. The only question was whether it would be too late.

3 2

Manuel sized up the man and woman sitting across his desk. He'd known who they were well before they flashed their badges. Out-of-towners were usually easy to spot. Especially when they wore suits.

"…and this is my partner, Special Agent Wilkins," the woman—who'd just introduced herself as Special Agent Howard—said. She had a slim build and frizzy red hair. Agent Wilkins, meanwhile, was a man whose body said former DI football player and whose buzzcut said former military.

"Thank you for coming," Manuel said. "We don't get many cases like this around here."

"That's not surprising," said Agent Howard. "Serial murderers aren't as common these days as they were in the eighties and nineties. And it was rare even then."

Manuel thought it odd how she said "serial murderers" instead of the more colloquial term "serial killers." Like she felt the need to distinguish herself from the average true crime junkie.

"We don't know for a fact yet that's what we're dealing with, though," Agent Wilkins added. "Without any bodies, we could be looking at a serial kidnapper. But that's even more rare."

Manuel thought of Zion. The chance he might still be alive caused his heart to flutter even though his mind knew it almost certainly wasn't true.

Agent Howard must have noticed; she offered a compassionate smile. "We were informed that one of the missing persons is your nephew, Sheriff. I want to extend my condolences and let you know that the Bureau is going to do everything in its power to find whoever took him."

"And what is it, if you don't mind me asking, that you're going to do?"

"We're with the Behavioral Analysis Unit," Agent Wilkins said. "Have you heard of it?"

"In passing," Manuel said.

"We analyze crimes to create a psychological profile of the person who committed them," Agent Howard said. "It helps narrow down the suspect list. And predict what they're going to do next."

"What can you tell me about this one?" Manuel asked.

"Not much, at the moment," Agent Howard said. "We're going to need some time to research all the missing persons. Conduct interviews. It's a process."

"What we can say right now," said Agent Wilkins, "is that the list of missing persons connected to the vehicles you found is quite interesting."

"How so?" Manuel asked.

"Well, for one, they're from all over Texas," Agent Wilkins said. "And yet the vehicles were all found in the same location. Means the perp probably lives somewhere nearby, but they've got a lot of range when it comes to their targets."

"Yeah," Manuel said. He'd put this much together already himself. "What else?"

"The victim profiles are all over the map too," Agent Howard said. "You've got men and women, age twenty to seventy-nine. Two of them were a married couple."

"And that tells you what?"

"It tells us the perp doesn't seem to have a type. We'll have to take a closer look into their background, see if we can find any commonalities, but for now it appears they're all just victims of opportunity. Which isn't unheard of when you're dealing with spontaneous killings. Think someone like Son of Sam. He didn't choose his victims ahead of time. They were just in the wrong place at the wrong time. But our perp is driving all over the state, convincing their victims to either follow them back or give them a ride, then dumping the vehicles. With that level of planning and carefulness, you'd expect them to be particular about who they target as well."

"So, who are we looking for here?" Manuel asked. "Some kind of psychopath? Sexual sadist?"

"That's the thing," Agent Wilkins said. "If there was a sexual element to these crimes, it'd be even more likely that the perp would display some kind of preference in their victims. Even assuming they have bisexual attractions, there's still the age ranges, physical differences, the differences in socioeconomic status..."

"It's very unusual," Agent Howard finished. "Which is part of the reason the Bureau is so interested."

"What do you need from me?" Manuel asked.

"Just your cooperation," she said. "That and an open exchange of information."

"And maybe an office where we could set up shop," Agent Wilkins said. "If you have one."

"There's the basement," Manuel said, a bit abashed. "I apologize. In case you can't tell, this place could use a renovation."

"The basement's fine," Agent Howard said. "If you'll just show us the way."

Manuel held the office door for them, then led them down the west corridor to the basement stairs. He turned on the overhead lights and took stock of the place, relieved to see it was in tidy enough shape. There was a trio of desks arranged in a rough semicircle, each with an outdated computer sitting on top it.

"I'll get those moved out of here for you," Manuel said, gesturing at the technological dinosaurs.

"It's alright," Agent Wilkins said, setting his laptop on the desk facing the doorway. "They're not in the way."

"That should be everything for now," Agent Howard said. "Thank you, Sheriff. We're going to start making some calls. See if we can get some interviews set up."

Manuel left them to it. Part of him wanted to stick around and watch them work. When he'd told Agent Wilkins that he'd heard of the BAU in passing, he'd meant he'd heard about it on TV. *Criminal Minds,* to be exact, back when he and Violet used to watch the show together. He'd be lying if he said he wasn't curious to see the real thing in action. Then again, the real thing probably wasn't all that exciting to watch. And he'd just be underfoot either way.

"Hey, Sheriff," Mrs. Henly—as of three weeks ago, the new department secretary—said, catching him in the hallway. "I've got a Detective Stark from DPS on hold for you."

Probably wanted to bitch about him calling in the feds so soon. But Manuel didn't care. There was a predator on the loose in his county. An honest-to-God psychopath, and one smart enough not to get caught yet at that. One who had taken Manuel's nephew. Other than catching the bastard, getting justice for Zion and closure for his sister, there wasn't a single thing left in the world that he really gave a damn about.

3 3

"Would you hand Momma that bag of mulch?" Charlotte asked, rubbing at an ache in her lower back as she stood.

Malachi retrieved the bag from the trunk of Charlotte's SUV, swinging it back and forth while he walked as though it were light as a handbag, even though the text printed near its bottom read "60 lbs."

"Please try not to bust it," Charlotte said. Malachi stopped swinging the bag and set it down on the ground.

The two of them had been working for the past hour to spread mulch around the trees and flower beds in the yard. Sometimes, Malachi complained about having to help out with chores around the house. But not today. If anything, he'd been quiet all morning. A lot quieter than normal.

"Something bothering you, kiddo?" Charlotte asked. Truth be told, she'd been working up the nerve. Bracing for the answer.

"I been thinking about some things," Malachi said, hands in his pockets. Charlotte stopped ripping open the mulch bag and lifted her head to look up at him. With the sun behind him, his face was a valley of shadows.

"Whatcha been thinking about?"

"I think I want to see the guy in the basement again."

Charlotte winced at the stab of dread in her chest. This is exactly what she'd expected him to say. It was early—he usually went at least a few months between feedings—but all the signs were there.

"Is it time again already?" she asked, her voice weaker than she'd meant for it to be.

"Time for what, Momma?"

"Time for you to eat."

Malachi shook his head. And Charlotte straightened a little, relieved but even more surprised. "No," he said. "I'm not hungry yet."

"Then why do you want to see the guy in the basement again?"

Malachi's eyes dropped to his shoes. He kicked gently at a clod of mulch, toppling it over into the grass. "Just 'cause."

"I don't think that's a good idea," Charlotte said. It couldn't be a good idea. But the way Malachi sighed told her he wasn't going to leave it at that.

"I want to play with him again."

Some line about not playing with one's food landed at the tip of Charlotte's tongue, but she dismissed it. "It's not safe, Malachi," she said instead.

Malachi huffed again, even more dramatic this time. "That's what you *always* say."

"Well…because it's true."

Was it, though? It was her go-to excuse, that was for sure; Malachi was right about that. But Charlotte honestly didn't know what was safe and unsafe anymore. What was right and wrong.

"I'm a big kid now, Momma," Malachi said. It was probably something he'd heard a kid on some show tell his or her parents. Though Charlotte would bet that kid wasn't actually as large as a full-grown man when they said it. It seemed to have more weight coming from someone so physically mature, even if his voice did crack a little when he spoke.

"I know you are. It's not that."

"What is it then?"

Charlotte exhaled. She lacked the mental clarity to explain it to him in a way he could understand. And perhaps the patience, too. "Because I said so, alright?"

Malachi stared at her. Even with the shadows on his face and the glare of the sun behind him, she could see the sudden intensity in his eyes. "That's not fair."

"Listen to me…" Charlotte started. Then suddenly she felt a tingle at the back of her head—a sharp pins and needles sensation horribly familiar even though she hadn't felt it in years.

No.

Malachi forced the word into her thoughts like an ice pick to the skull. Charlotte grimaced, then gathered herself and glared back at him, rising to her feet even though it didn't change the fact she still had to look up at him.

"Malachi Mallory! I have told you before to *never* do that to me. You are going to listen—"

NO!

Charlotte stumbled and almost tripped over the mulch bag. Her vision swirled, then a piercing ring filled her ears. Malachi was breathing heavy. His chest heaved, and his fists were clenched into balls at his side. For a fleeting moment, for the first time since he was born, Charlotte feared for her own life more than his.

"Malachi," she wheezed.

Then he was off. Sprinting away at a wholly unnatural speed. She reached for him, but he was already across the yard by the time her fingers brushed the spot he'd been. Charlotte watched him, holding her breath. Hoping he wouldn't turn down the road toward the highway. It was like the nightmare that plagued her sleep almost every night brought to life. And there was nothing she could do to stop it.

Mercifully, Malachi didn't follow the road. He kept running straight instead, across the fields and into the woods on the south end of her property. As far as Charlotte knew, he could run for miles in that direction and not come across so much as a single neighboring home. It was a horrifying thought in its own right, but much less so than the alternative.

As she stood there contemplating whether she should follow him, knowing full well that catching him was hopeless, the tingling sensation at the back of her head returned. Tears dropped from Charlotte's eyes and soaked into the thirsty Texas soil as his voice crept into her mind—weaker and much more distant this time, but just as awful.

You can't tell me what to do anymore, Momma.

Charlotte lowered herself to the ground on trembling legs and cried until her eyes ran dry. Because if he meant it, then he was right.

216

34

Zion cleared his throat and wiped his eyes with the tips of his fingers. He felt woozy all of a sudden. Something close to drunk, even though he hadn't tasted a drop since waking up in The Bitch's basement. Sitting near him on the couch—much too near for Zion's liking—the boy kept staring at him with those strange, unnerving eyes.

It was the second time this week Malachi had visited him. And that's not counting the visit ten days ago—the one that pissed his mom off so much she pointed a gun at Zion's head. Zion wasn't sure what had changed since then, and Malachi had just shrugged it off when he asked about whether she'd be mad.

At first, Zion had seen it as an opportunity. He still did—winning the kid's friendship was his best hope of survival. But the feeling he'd been left with following Malachi's most recent visit had lingered ever since. It was like a fogginess in his head. A sense of confusion that lasted all hours.

Now that the boy was back again, the feeling was stronger than ever. It seemed like the room should be spinning given how disoriented he felt, but it wasn't. His view was one of Malachi's motionless body and frozen expression. More like a photograph than living, breathing reality. A moment in time that stretched on and on.

"Who are you?" Malachi asked after what felt like ages.

"My name is Zion."

Wasn't it? And hadn't he told him that already? Zion couldn't be sure. On either account, really.

Malachi touched his leg. His fingers felt like ice cubes and prickled Zion's skin. But he couldn't pull away. Not in the sense that he didn't want to be rude but in the sense that he *physically* couldn't. As if the boy's touch had turned his legs to stone.

"Are you my friend?" Malachi asked.

"Yes," Zion said. The word rolled right off his tongue. Was it even him speaking anymore? The splitting throb in the back of his head was all he could think about, and yet his lips kept right on moving anyway whenever Malachi asked him questions.

"Are we going to play together all the time?"

"Yes," Zion said again. Again, it felt he had no choice.

Malachi grinned wide. The sight of his teeth made the queasiness in Zion's stomach spike, and he swallowed to keep its contents from coming up.

"Are you going to do everything I tell you to do?" he asked.

No is what Zion wanted to scream. He wanted to put his hands around the kid's throat and squeeze the life out of whatever wicked thing lived behind those eyes. But he could hardly even formulate the thought anymore. Much less act on it.

"Yesunngh." He felt his mouth forming the word against his will and fought to stop it. When groaning didn't work, he bit his tongue hard enough for it to taste itself.

Are you… The boy's voice came from inside Zion's head now, yet ten times louder than before. *Going to…do everything.….I tell you?*

"Yes!" Zion shrieked, the pain squashing any will to resist.

Malachi grinned again and clapped his hands. Zion closed his eyes, held his breath, and tried to ignore the feeling that his entire mind—entire world—was crumbling like sandcastle walls.

"Who are you?" Malachi asked, his grin disappearing in an instant as the cold seriousness returned to his eyes.

"I…I'm…"

"Let's call you, hmmm…how 'bout Jellybean?"

Zion didn't even register what he'd said. He was somewhere else now. Floating. Drifting. Watching this absurd scene play out like a spectator in the auditorium rather than an actor on the stage.

"Jellybean! My friend Jellybean. Do you like it?"

"Yes," someone said.

But it wasn't him. Not anymore.

3 5

Standing near the back of a large conference room packed with officers from his department, Hooper Valley PD, and DPS, Manuel checked his watch. Agent Wilkins and Agent Howard were taking their time getting here. They'd been taking their time the past three weeks, too. Though, to be fair, Manuel couldn't really say whether three weeks was a long time or not without knowing what they were actually doing.

Supposedly, the two of them had a report to present. A complete psychological profile of the unknown subject the entire state of Texas was hunting for. Manuel, like every other cop in the room, was keen to hear it – even if he did have his doubts about its usefulness.

At last, nearly ten more minutes later, Howard and Wilkins walked through the door. Agent Howard set her laptop on the podium and began fussing with it while Agent Wilkins stood by her side. Conversation in the room lowered to a hum as everyone watched the two of them—some curious, some suspicious, and almost all of them impatient.

"Good morning," Agent Howard said. "I apologize for the delay."

Manuel waited for her to offer some excuse, but she never did. Both she and her partner looked a bit disheveled. Like they'd stayed up all night working the case. Or maybe up all night doing something else.

"What Agent Wilkins and I hope to do today is present you all with a profile of your UNSUB. One you can use to guide your investigation. This profile is based on a comprehensive analysis of the UNSUB's victims, their behaviors, and their patterns. While none of the theories we have compiled are absolute, they are based on solid science and careful analysis."

It was hot in the room. Whoever had set the thermostat had failed to account for how many warm bodies would be present. Agent Wilkins wiped his forehead with his sleeve before stepping up to the mic, and Manuel was starting to sweat too.

"First off," he said, "It is our belief that we are indeed dealing with a serial murderer. The lack of bodies makes it impossible to say for sure, but the odds that all…or any of the missing persons whose vehicles were found in Lake Kinley are still alive is exceedingly slim."

"I'm sure you all have already reached the same conclusion," Agent Howard added.

That was a safe bet if there ever was one, Manuel figured. He hoped the rest of this briefing would offer more value. Not just because of the time they'd be wasting if it didn't, but because, if this failed, he didn't know where to turn next.

"The UNSUB is what we call an organized killer," Agent Wilkins said. "Their attacks are carefully planned ahead of time as opposed to impulsive acts of violence. This is demonstrated by the long distances they traveled to capture their victims and the fact that they had a plan for disposing of the evidence."

"My partner says 'captured,'" Agent Howard said, "because it is our belief that all of the victims were transported to a second location before they were killed. This could have been done under coercion, or they could have been traveling with the UNSUB voluntarily."

"We believe the second possibility is more likely," Agent Wilkins said. "Michael Pelphrey, the first victim on the timeline, was a Desert Storm vet known to carry a handgun everywhere he went. The SMU students that went missing most recently were three large, healthy young men. Taking them by force would have been challenging and risky."

"Speaking of the victim profiles," Agent Howard said. "The diversity of the victims is by far the most interesting element of this case. Agent Wilkins and I have spent the last three weeks analyzing everything that is known about the eight missing persons connected to this case. We found almost no similarities between any of them. In fact, there is only one real commonality that all eight of them share, and that is the fact that they are all sexually attracted to women. Five of the eight victims were heterosexual men, four of them single, one married but with a history of infidelity. Mr. and Mrs. Schmidt were in an open relationship, and both were bisexual. And Becka Green was lesbian."

"This," Agent Howard continued. She cleared her throat a little. Like what was coming next would be hard for her to say. "This leads us to conclude that our UNSUB is a woman."

Manuel heard a couple scoffs and a lot of murmuring. It would've sounded strange—sounded like bullshit—to him as well if it weren't for the sudden fidget in his hands that said otherwise.

"I know what you're thinking," Agent Howard said. "Women account for only ten percent of serial murderers, but ten percent is not a negligible number."

"There are very few reasons why someone would willingly drive to a second location with a complete stranger," Agent Wilkins stepped in to add. "Sex is one of them. The theory that the UNSUB is female would also explain why the victims might not have felt threatened."

"We considered the possibility that the person doing the abducting might have been working for a second induvial," Agent Howard said. "It's uncommon, but psychopaths have been known to rope their girlfriends, wives, or even friends and family into helping them lure victims. But those kinds of relationships almost never remain stable for long, and our UNSUB has been doing this for over five years now."

"What's the motive?" someone in the crowd asked. Manuel couldn't see who.

"We don't know," Agent Howard said. And at this, another round of doubtful murmurs predictably ensued. "The vast majority of female serial murderers kill for financial gain. But there's no evidence to suggest that's the case here. It is extremely rare for women to kill for sexual gratification, and the lack of similarity between the victims makes it even more unlikely."

"We do have a theory, though," Agent Wilkins said. Manuel thought he caught a hint of a frown from Agent Howard as her partner said this and wondered if the *we* should have been an *I*.

"One possible motive is that the UNSUB is suffering from some form of psychotic delusions," he continued. "These could be ritualistic killings intended to serve some imagined religious purpose. Or the UNSUB could be convinced that they are mercy killings."

"We can't rule it out," Agent Howard said, mostly suppressing the doubt in her tone. "I do, however, want to note that there is a wide variety of reasons why people kill, and not all of them fit into clearly defined boxes. That said, it may be worth looking into women in this area who have a history of mental illness.

"And that actually brings me to our final point, which is that we do believe the UNSUB lives somewhere in the vicinity of where the vehicles were dumped. This is a fairly obvious conclusion. The logistical challenges that arise if we assume the UNSUB doesn't live relatively near Lake Kinley all but rule out the possibility."

"So," Agent Wilkins said, "here's what that leaves us with. We are looking for a female suspect, age twenty-one to sixty. She likely lives alone and somewhere within a thirty-mile radius of Lake Kinley. This would allow her to either walk home after dumping the vehicles or at least walk back into town and get a ride from there. She may have a history of mental illness and is likely to have a criminal record, though it's possible she stayed clean until the killings started. She is likely to be physically attractive and socially skilled despite being predominantly anti-social when she's not on the hunt."

"We go into all of these details more in-depth in our full report," Agent Howard said. "Which will be made available to everyone in this room. If any of you have any questions, we'd be happy to try and answer them."

There were a few questions. Hannah Renly, the Hooper Lake Chief of Police, asked about their level of confidence in this assessment, clearly not very confident herself. Someone else asked about what the killer was doing with the bodies. All the while, Manuel's nerves continued to simmer.

It took close to twenty minutes for everyone to filter out of the room. Manuel made sure he was the last to leave. He approached Agent Howard as she was zipping her laptop case.

"Can I have a word?" he asked.

"Of course," Agent Howard said, though Manuel could tell she was already bracing for more skepticism.

"That profile. Single woman, relatively young, lives alone, history of run-ins with law enforcement."

"Yes?" Agent Howard said.

"I know someone who fits it."

"Who?" Agent Wilkins asked, suddenly interested himself. They both were.

"Her name's Charlotte Mallory," Manuel said.

"Wait," Agent Howard said. "You mean Charlotte Mallory the romance author?"

"That's the one. Lives by herself on a ranch about fifteen miles out of town."

"You know her?" Agent Wilkins asked, looking at his partner.

"I've read some of her books," Agent Howard said. "I never paid attention to where she lived. What makes you think it's her, Sheriff? You know, just because someone writes about dark subject matter doesn't necessarily mean—"

"No, it's not that," Manuel said. "I first met Charlotte about five years ago. An elderly woman named Deborah Vickers was murdered in her living room while Ms. Mallory was out of the house. Whoever did it left her kid unharmed. Then a few years later, the kid goes missing. We never had a single break in either case."

"Interesting," Agent Howard said.

"Yeah, that's not the best part. She's also one of the last people known to have seen my nephew and the two other SMU boys. She spoke to them at The Sapphire Lounge the night they went missing."

"Have you talked with her?" Agent Wilkins asked.

"Yeah," Mauel said. "Her story is the boys left alone. Says her sister came and picked her up from the bar shortly after."

"And does the sister corroborate that story?" Agent Howard asked.

"She does."

"Think Ms. Mallory would agree to come in for a chat?" Agent Wilkins asked.

"To be honest, I'd a lot rather just go kick her door down," Manuel said. "The problem is Judge Hargrave is picky about the warrants he signs. I think it would take more than what we've got to get him on board, especially with her being the town celebrity."

"What's her sister's name?" Agent Howard asked.

"Lilibeth Wyatt. Lives with her husband and young boy in town."

"Maybe it would be better to talk to her again instead," Agent Howard offered. "If we can get her to change her story, there's not a judge in the country who wouldn't sign that warrant."

"Showing up unannounced would definitely be ideal," Agent Wilkins said. "We get a warrant first, we could turn the whole place upside down before she had a chance to hide any evidence."

"I like the sound of that," Manuel said.

"We'd like to be there, if that's alright," Agent Howard said. "When you talk with Mrs. Wyatt."

"That'd be fine."

"When do you think we could arrange it?" Agent Howard asked. "The quicker we move on this, the better."

Manuel checked his watch. It was only a quarter past ten, several hours still before Lilibeth would have to go pick her kid up from school. "You two free right now?"

36

Charlotte was sick to her stomach. So physically affected by the dread eating at her heart that she'd thrown up twice already. Or dry heaved, more like. Hard to throw anything up when you haven't swallowed anything down all day.

She'd known it was coming for a while. But this morning, Malachi had made it clear. He was hungry again. Or getting there. And Zion was no longer on the menu. Charlotte still didn't know exactly what Malachi had done to him, what he wanted with him, but he wanted him alive.

That meant Charlotte had no choice but to hunt again. And little time to prepare herself for the wretched task ahead.

In fact, she planned to go out this very night. Who's to say whether she'd be successful; that's why it was always important to start trying as soon as Malachi gave her the indication.

"I can do it, Momma," he'd told her earlier today. "If you don't want to." Maybe he'd sensed her anxiety, but the offer certainly didn't make it any better.

It wasn't normal that he would need to feed again so early. Whatever he had done to Zion wasn't normal either. But, thinking of this, Charlotte couldn't help but laugh as the tears streaked down her cheeks. *Normal* was a word that had never applied to her life, and certainly not the last eight years.

It was unsustainable. A runaway train that could only end one way. It might have been a relief, knowing it would all end soon, if she had only herself to think about. But there were others. Malachi, and so many others.

It was time to focus, because time was ticking. Abeline—her hunting ground for the night—was an hour-and-a-half drive away, and she'd need to leave soon if she was going to get there by dusk. Standing on a stool to reach it, Charlotte opened the cabinet above her stove. It was where she kept her wine glasses. And, tucked behind them, a burnt orange pill bottle a quarter of the way full with 10 mg Valium tablets.

Satisfied that there were plenty of them left to get the job done (despite the fact she'd been filching them for herself more and more often lately), Charlotte closed the cabinet and headed outside.

The walk to the barn went by in a blur, adrenaline pushing her along much faster than her ordinary gait. When she spotted the thing she'd come here to check, her stomach started flipping again.

The ball and chain she'd welded together herself several years ago still sat near the center of the sawdust floor. It had taken Malachi's help to get it there, and he was the only one who'd ever managed to move it an inch since. Charlotte knelt and checked its shackle. She tested the hinges to make sure they weren't rusty but avoided locking it all the way.

A crow squawked somewhere just outside the barn, making her heart leap. Charlotte set the shackle down and hurried away from the place. Other than storing excess hay, the barn had only one purpose. Because of that, she avoided it as much as possible. She had never believed in ghosts, but the spirits of all those who had died here still haunted the place in a less literal sense. They haunted her mind every time she stepped foot on this blood-soaked ground.

She tried not to picture their faces as she made her way back to the house. Tried and failed, like usual. Some of them had been smiling and laughing when they met her. Some had seemed lost and melancholy. None of them deserved what she did to them.

There'd been a time—back when she was first coming to grips with what she would have to do—that Charlotte had envisioned herself becoming a sort of vigilante. Going after only those who had it coming. Drug dealers and rapists and people the world would be better off without.

That had been laughably naïve. She wasn't Batman, for crying out loud. It wasn't like she could just drop into a dark alley and expect to find some crook stealing an old woman's purse. And she'd probably just get herself killed even if she did.

She'd eventually accepted that opportunity would have to be her only compass. Any other means of justifying whom she chose—any sin or shortcoming she could point to—was always woefully inadequate. No one was blameless, and if she had to be their executioner, she refused to be their judge as well.

Charlotte checked her phone for the time. It was almost 5 o'clock. She grabbed her purse off the kitchen table and made sure it held all the items she needed—her keys, a second bottle of Valium, and, just in case shit really hit the fan, the 9mm pistol. She checked her makeup in her compact mirror, then headed upstairs.

Malachi's bedroom door was open, and she saw him lying in bed, staring up at the ceiling with his hands folded over his stomach.

"Hey," she said, stepping into the room. Malachi glanced at her but didn't say anything. "I'm about to go out for a while, okay?"

Malachi nodded. He rubbed at his temples and clenched his eyes like he had a headache. Then he sighed and opened them again.

"You need anything before I go?"

"No," he said. "Just hurry."

The pleading in his tone made Charlotte feel cold inside. How had it escalated this quickly? Not even two full months had passed since his last feeding. And now they were nearing the desperation zone already.

"Just stay here, alright," Charlotte said. "I don't care if you go outside, but don't wander far."

"Only to the end of the driveway," Malachi said.

"That's right."

He knew the rules—it wasn't a question of that. It was how much longer he would continue to follow them that set Charlotte's nerves simmering. One failure on her part to deliver what he needed in time, one act of childish rebellion, and it would end in cataclysm.

"I'll be back soon," she said, then headed out the door.

37

BEFORE

Charlotte took a long breath and ground her teeth hard enough to hurt. She had to stop her hands from shaking. It would never work if she didn't. But it seemed as if they'd formed minds of their own.

She gripped the steering wheel at ten and two. That helped a little. Maybe if she kept them there, she could keep them still.

Her car's headlights and a streetlamp on the sidewalk illuminated the empty road ahead. She was somewhere on the south side of the city, the hour having grown so late that there were few other vehicles on the road.

Underneath the streetlamp was a wooden bench, painted green but in desperate need of a new coat. A man lay stretched across it with a blanket over his legs. Through the windshield, Charlotte could just make out his scraggly beard to confirm it was indeed a man, and an older one too by the splotches of gray.

She crept slowly down the road, barely pressing the accelerator. She was stalling, still considering whether she should stop or keep driving.

She'd struck out all night at the clubs and bars. Coming all the way to Dallas had seemed like a good way to distance herself from the crime she intended to commit tonight, but she'd not counted on how difficult it would be to get someone to agree to a two-and-a-half-hour drive to a middle-of-nowhere destination. No matter how much she threw herself at them. When the men she'd succeeded at seducing had balked and mentioned hotels or their place just a few blocks away, Charlotte didn't have a good response.

Now it was almost one in the morning. Malachi was home alone. And hungry. So hungry his eyes betrayed his desperation. If she didn't return home with...something to feed him, there was no telling what would happen.

Charlotte eased off the accelerator a little more and rolled to a stop next to the bench. The man sleeping on it still didn't stir. She began to wonder if he was even alive. Maybe he'd pushed the plunger a little too far this time and fell asleep once and for all beneath the cold city lights.

Charlotte rolled down the window. She cleared her throat, and the man stirred just a little.

"Hey," she said and instantly hated how her voice sounded.

The man rolled over. Charlotte got a good look at his face in the yellow-orange lamplight. There were wrinkles on his leathery skin and an L-shaped scar above his left eyebrow. He squinted at her when he opened his eyes. Charlotte couldn't tell if it was the light or nearsightedness. Or maybe he just couldn't believe what they were seeing.

"What's your name?" she asked.

"Robert, ma'am. Can I help ya?"

He stood up then, and Charlotte's heart began to pound even faster. She gripped the wheel tight enough to choke it and bounced her leg up and down out of sight beneath the steering column.

"Actually," she said. "I was wondering if I could help you?"

Robert scrunched up his face. It looked as though the cobwebs of sleep weren't all the way dusted out yet, and this strange interaction was already more than he could handle at such a late hour.

"I have a ranch," she went on. "About two hours from here. If you're looking for some work and a place to stay for a while, I could use the help."

Robert stared at her for a bit before he answered. "So what you're saying is that you're driving 'round Dallas...in the middle of the night...looking for a *ranch hand*?"

"It's, umm...a special kind of ranch," Charlotte said, thinking on her feet.

Robert thought about it for a beat, then grinned, catching her drift. "You're growing something Uncle Sam don't approve of out there, aren't ya?"

"You could say that."

Robert sniffed. Charlotte watched him pick his blanket back up and begin spreading it over the bench. "Well, more power to ya, ma'am. But I don't know nothing 'bout any of that."

"I can pay you," Charlotte said. She unzipped her purse and produced a $100 bill. "This now, just for going with me, then $800 a week until the harvest is over."

He took a long look at the bill in her hand. Charlotte realized he could probably just snatch it—and the rest of the money in her purse too—if he really wanted to, and she wondered if he was thinking the same thing. But she kept it extended out the window anyway.

"My back ain't so good anymore," Robert said.

"It's not hard work," Charlotte said. "Just mildly risky work."

Robert chuckled. "You got some grit in ya, don't ya?"

More than she ever knew she did, that was for sure. "Comes with a bed and three meals a day too. Then, if you want, I can bring you back here as soon as the job's done."

"This ain't some kind of a trick, is it?" He still eyed the bill in her hand as he spoke, his expression a mix of distrust and desire.

"No tricks," Charlotte said. "If you change your mind, you're free to leave anytime. Lord knows I wouldn't be able to stop you."

"Well hell," Robert said. "This might be the strangest thing that's ever happened to me, but I say you got yourself a deal."

Charlotte handed him the one-hundred-dollar bill. She half expected him to turn right back around and take off with it and had already decided there was nothing she could do if he did. Instead, he tucked the bill into his shirt pocket and got into the car.

"Nice ride," he said, running his fingers across the leather dash.

"Thanks," Charlotte said, though she hardly cared anymore. She'd bought the vehicle two years ago with the advance from *Tempting the Devil*. Back then, she'd been thrilled to own something so nice, but that was before she knew what it would really cost.

She put the car in drive and accelerated away, in a hurry to be out of there before someone saw her. The streets were empty, and the odds were likely that no one would ever go looking for this man. Still, she knew that after tonight, she'd be looking over her shoulder for the rest of her life.

38

Casting a glance up at the blazing sun, Manuel sighed and knocked on the door again, a little harder than the first time. "Mrs. Wyatt, this is the Sheriff's Department. We need to talk to you."

Her car was in the driveway. And though he wasn't positive, Manuel thought he'd heard a TV playing as they were walking up the porch.

He waited a while, reached out to knock again, then a voice from behind the door stayed his hand.

"I don't have anything more to tell you, Sheriff."

"Mrs. Wyatt, can you open the door?" When she didn't respond, he said, "We know about Charlotte. We know you haven't been entirely truthful with us, too. If you won't talk to me, I'm not gonna be able to protect you from what comes next."

Another long moment passed with no response. Manuel looked back at the FBI agents standing just behind him and frowned. If she refused to talk, there was nothing they could do. Not right now at least.

But then came the sound every cop not holding a warrant in their hands loves to hear—the screech of a lock retracting. The door opened, and Lilibeth Wyatt peered out at them.

"Who are they?" she asked, nodding at the agents.

"My name's Special Agent Howard," the woman said, stepping up next to Manuel. "That's my partner, Special Agent Wilkins. We're with the Federal Bureau of Investigation."

"Jesus Christ," Lilibeth muttered.

"Can we come in?" Manuel asked.

Lilibeth didn't say yes, but she left the door wide open when she turned away. Manuel waited for a second, then followed her inside. He paused in the kitchen while she poured a glass of wine. When she'd filled it nearly to the brim, she sat down at the kitchen table. Manuel and the FBI agents sat down across from her.

"We need to talk to you again about the night of November 17th," Manuel said. "For the sake of you and your family, you really need to be honest with us this time."

Lilibeth laced her fingers together to stop them from fidgeting. She'd been nervous the first time Manuel came by. Nervous and annoyed the second. Now, she looked terrified.

"We're going to record this interview, if you don't mind," Agent Wilkins said, then he pressed the bright red circle on his digital recorder without waiting for whether she minded or not. That was new too, and Manuel caught her staring at the recorder like it was a time bomb sitting on her kitchen table.

"I want to revisit the statement you gave about that night," Manuel said. "You said you picked your sister up from The Sapphire Lounge around eleven. That right?"

Lilibeth bit at the corner of her lip. "Are you asking if that's what I said or…"

"I'm asking if it's correct."

She hesitated. Manuel could clearly see the calculations going on in her mind as she decided whether to double down or fold. It excited him, but it also made him feel like kicking himself for not pressing her this hard sooner.

"Be honest with me, starting right now, and I'll make sure there aren't any charges brought against you." That was a half-truth; in reality, it would be up to the DA more than him.

But it worked anyway. Lilibeth crumpled, erupting into sobs and a shaking fit that wracked her entire body. Agent Howard switched seats and gave the woman a few tepid pats on the back.

Manuel waited patiently. When the sobs gave way to sniffles, he asked her one more time. "Did you pick Charlotte up from The Sapphire Lounge the night of November 17th?"

"No," Lilibeth croaked.

"Were you with her at all that night?"

"No. She called the next morning and asked for a ride to go pick up her car. Then she told me if anyone asked to say I'd picked her up the night before."

"Why would she tell you to lie?" Agent Howard asked.

"I don't know," said Lilibeth. "I promise I don't. Charlotte...she has problems. I don't know exactly what they are or what she's got herself into, but..."

"But you lied for her anyway," Manuel said.

"I'm sorry," Lilibeth said, still sniffling.

"What makes you think she's involved with something?" Agent Wilkins asked.

Lilibeth shook her head. "I said I didn't know."

"But you suspect it," he pressed.

Lilibeth took a deep, shaky breath. "It's just that it's not the first time she wanted me to lie about where she was. No one ever asked any of the times before. But now there's all this and those missing boys, and…oh God, what have I done?"

"Has she told you anything?" Manuel asked. "She ever mention anything about those missing people?"

Lilibeth shook her head. "We don't talk much anymore." She paused. Manuel could tell she was on the verge of saying more. "But, umm… there is one more thing."

"What's that?"

"Her son. Malachi. Do you remember him?"

"Yeah," Manuel said. "Been missing a little over four years now."

"I saw him," Lilibeth blurted out.

"When?" Manuel asked. For the first time since this interview started, she'd managed to stun him.

"Last fall. I can't remember now why I even went out there. But I knocked on the door, and when she didn't answer, I just let myself in. And I saw him, Sheriff. He ran upstairs as soon as he noticed me, but I'm sure it was him."

Manuel shared a look with the two FBI agents. He'd told them the basics of his history with Charlotte Mallory on the drive over. Now, both of them looked just as floored as he was. Agent Howard gave him a small nod. Manuel knew what it meant; it meant they had all they needed.

"Thank you, Mrs. Wyatt." he said. "That's everything for now."

"What's going to happen to her?" Lilibeth asked.

"I don't know yet."

Lilibeth opened her mouth to speak, then closed it again. She closed her eyes too, squeezing out a tear from each one. No telling how guilty she felt—either for turning in her own blood or not doing it a lot sooner. Probably a mix of both.

"You did the right thing," he said. But Lilibeth couldn't bear to look at him.

"Now where?" Agent Howard asked once they were out of the house.

"Now we go get a warrant," Manuel said.

39

Harvey Johnson took a long swig of his double whiskey and Coke and felt it go straight to his head. He had a long way to go before he reached the point he needed to, but it was early still. Outside the bar's glass door, twilight was just starting to settle in.

He fiddled at the ring on his finger, contemplating taking it off and slipping it into his pocket. But then again, the woman down the bar—the one who'd been giving him looks the past twenty minutes—had surely noticed the ring already as much as he'd been messing with it. And if she had seen it, she didn't seem to care.

Harvey didn't care anymore either. Not about the ring or the woman who'd put it there nine years ago. Well, scratch that. He would have cared about *that* woman, if she still existed. That woman didn't treat sex like a chore or him like a whipping post. He did blame himself almost as much as her, though; they say flowers bloom when you water them, but he'd never had much of a green thumb.

And then, the very night he finally accepts that he doesn't love her anymore, here's this lady at the bar, doe eyes looking at him in a way no woman (certainly not his wife) had looked at him in years.

She was gorgeous. Out of his league by any sane person's measure. And she was coming toward him.

Harvey polished off the rest of his drink and watched her approach. When he met her eyes, it set his heart pounding.

"Mind if I join you?" she asked. Her voice sounded exactly like he expected it to. Like sugar and velvet and sin.

"Sure," he said, desperate to not sound desperate.

"What's your name?"

"Harvey. What about you?"

Did she hesitate then? Think about giving him a fake one? Or maybe she was just being coy. Harvey was so out of practice, he could hardly tell.

"I'm Charlotte," she said.

"Can I buy you a drink?" he asked, even though the glass of white wine in her hand was mostly full.

"I'm alright for now," she said. "But thank you."

She touched his thigh then, her fingers lingering for an exhilarating second. Even through the denim of his blue jeans, it felt electrifying.

"Drinking alone tonight?" she asked.

"Yeah," Harvey said. He caught her looking at the wedding band on his finger and couldn't stave off the red warmth rising in his cheeks. "It's a long story."

"I haven't cared much for stories lately anyway," Charlotte said.

"What do you care about?" he asked.

"Experiences."

Harvey studied her. He wasn't misreading this, was he? No, surely not. Even a dope like him couldn't possibly misread signals this strong.

The only question was what he was going to do about it. He'd not come here with the intention of cheating on his wife. What he'd come here for was to get shitfaced and forget she existed for a few hours.

He could do it the right way. At least file the papers and move out before he saw other women. But then, there'd never be this moment again. He'd never be here at this bar with this woman anytime but now.

"Want to get out of here?" Charlotte asked. Harvey could hardly believe what was happening.

"Moving pretty fast, don't you think?" It was a stupid thing to say. The kind of thing that could blow his chances. But Harvey needed time to think. It was moving fast for him, that's for sure, and if he didn't take a step back and consider now, it would quickly be too late.

To his relief, she only shrugged and smiled a little instead of taking it as rejection. "I know what I want when I see it, Harvey."

Harvey had to stifle a bewildered chuckle. Because what was it exactly that she'd seen in *him*? He was visibly out of shape, mildly attractive on his best day, and today was not that day. And while he did have money, nothing about the way he was dressed tonight would suggest it.

He almost asked her. But that would have been even more stupid than the last thing he said. And typical, too, he thought, scolding himself. Maybe if he'd had just an ounce of self-belief back in his younger years, he wouldn't have settled for the first woman that gave him attention.

"Where would we go?" he asked.

"I'm guessing your place is no good," Charlotte said.

Harvey shook his head. For the first time, he felt a pang of guilt when he thought of his wife at home in the house they'd kept together for the better part of a decade.

"I live about an hour or so from here," she said. "I know it's a bit of a drive. But, turns out I'm actually needing a ride anyway."

"How'd you get here?" Harvey asked.

"A friend. But she had something come up. I told her I could take a cab home, but, now that I'm thinking about it, I'm not sure I could even find one that would take me that far."

"It'd be a hell of a fare if they did."

"That's what I'm afraid of."

Harvey thought about it for a moment. Long enough for the silence between them to begin growing awkward. Then he took a deep breath and said the words that would drive a stake through the heart of his dying marriage.

"I can give you a lift."

"That's very kind of you," Charlotte said. Then, leaning in, "I promise I'll make it worth your time."

Harvey led her out of the bar to his Audi Q5 parked near the corner of the lot. The next thing he knew, she was in the passenger seat beside him, the expensive smell of her perfume filling the cabin.

"You'll want to get on I-35," she said, pointing at the exit ahead. Harvey turned his attention back to the road and did his best to keep it there.

For the next hour, they cruised down the interstate. Charlotte didn't talk much the rest of the way, though he tried his best to keep the conversation flowing. Maybe he was just being pessimistic—that old self-doubt creeping in again—but it seemed almost as if she'd lost interest the moment she got into his car.

It might be for the better, he thought. Not that he had any intentions of patching things up with Kaytlin at the moment, but if all he did was bring this woman home and drop her off, then he wouldn't have to live with the shame the rest of his years.

Only the regret. He let out an intentional sigh, but Charlotte didn't seem to notice. He turned on the radio and spun the dial until it landed on a country station that came in clear.

"This alright?"

"It's fine," she said.

Had he done something to upset her? Harvey tried to think if there was anything he'd said but came up blank. Whatever was bothering her, he decided it likely had nothing to do with him. In fact, her approaching him like she did, getting into his car, was probably a symptom of whatever wore on her mind, not its cause.

"You need to take the next exit," she said.

Harvey saw a green sign on the side of the interstate that said "Exit 43: Hooper Valley—1 mile."

"Hooper Valley," he said. "Hey, that's near where they found all those cars in the lake, right?"

Charlotte didn't say anything. She stared out the passenger window so that all he could see of her face was her reflection in the glass.

"Just so you know," Harvey said, considering his words carefully. "Just because I drove you all this way don't mean I think you owe me anything. I can drop you off and go on home, if that's what you want."

Charlotte looked at him and forced a smile. He could tell it was forced by the way it never touched her eyes, and he felt a strange chill.

"You'll turn left at the light. Then it's just a few more miles."

Harvey slowed the Audi down and took Exit 43. He waited at the light and turned left onto a two-lane highway. The clock on the dash read ten minutes after eight, which meant "about an hour" had turned into an hour and a half already. The whole night had turned into something different, in fact. At this point, he was just ready to get her out of his car and go home. She may or may not have changed her mind, but Harvey was quickly changing his.

"It's your next right," Charlotte said a few miles later. "That gravel road up ahead."

Harvey turned where she told him to. The pine forest on either side of the road swallowed his headlights, and the sound of rocks crunching beneath his tires seemed impossibly loud.

Harvey cleared his throat. "I don't want you to take this the wrong way," he said. "But I think I'm just gonna drop you off and head back. This, uhh…this was a mistake."

Charlotte's eyes widened. They actually widened—as if losing out on a night with him, Harvey Johnson the middle-aged software engineer—was something to be dismayed about. Far from finding it flattering, it only creeped him out more.

"No…" she said.

"No?"

"I just mean, you drove all this way. I'd feel bad if—"

"Like I said…" Harvey started. Then he trailed off. There were lights up ahead. Lots of them. Not just any kind of lights either. These were flashing red and blue. The "cherries and berries" he'd heard them called one time on some police show. Made sense that the memory would come to him now; TV was the only place he'd ever seen so many cop cars in one spot before.

"*Oh no,*" he heard Charlotte say. Before he could peel his eyes away from the scene in front of him, she was out the door and running across the headlights' beams.

Harvey hesitated for a while, paralyzed by wonder. Then it struck him that it isn't very often life gives you a bright, flashing sign to turn around and run the hell away. Much less a dozen of them. Peeling out so fast his tires sprayed the gravel, Harvey swerved his car around and drove all the way home without stopping.

40

"What's the call, Sheriff?" Deputy Rodgers asked. He, along with Manuel, the FBI agents, and a handful of other deputies all gathered around Charlotte Mallory's porch. The door was locked, and no one was answering. But that was nothing the metal battering ram cradled in Deputy Rodgers's thick arms couldn't solve in short order.

"We're going in," Manuel said. There could have been value in waiting for Ms. Mallory to return, but he wasn't waiting any longer. Being back on this ranch again—especially after what Lilibeth had told them—had his nerves on fire.

"Yes, sir," Deputy Rodgers said.

The sound of the ram smashing into the wood made Manuel flinch. Made him flinch like a damn schoolgirl in a spook house. He hoped none of his officers had noticed. But, then again, most of them seemed just as spooked. Something was wrong here. They could all feel it.

The ram struck the door again hard enough to shake its frame. The wood caved and splintered beneath the impact. One more blow and it swung open.

Manuel was the first to go inside. He walked through the entryway and scanned the living room. It looked tidy for the most part, nothing out of sorts. Except there on the floor next to the sofa was a plastic toy. Some sort of robot action figure, scuffed and worn from years of play. Hard play. Like the kind little boys are known for.

At one point in time, there'd been a disemboweled body in that same spot. The memory of it came back to Manuel suddenly, vivid as a vison, and his hairs stiffened.

"Spread out," he instructed his deputies. "Look for the kid. You see anything suspicious, you radio it in." A couple of them headed up the stairs. The rest fanned out downstairs and began going from room to room.

Manuel had held a briefing before they left, but it had lived up to the "brief" part of the word; by the time Judge Hargrave got back from the golf course and around to signing the warrant, the day was nearly over. He'd been in a rush to get here, even though he couldn't say why.

"We got a locked door over here," Deputy Hale called out. "Padlocked."

"Go get the grinder," Manuel instructed Deputy Rickard. He returned a minute later with the cordless tool in hand and followed Manuel through the living room to a hallway connecting the kitchen. Deputy Hale stood near the center of the hall next to a door with a thick bolt and padlock holding it shut. The basement door, if memory served him. Manuel had seen it before, the last time he was in this house. It seemed strange even then, with its dual locks. Now, it seemed damn near sinister.

"Open it," Manuel instructed. Deputy Rickard set the grinder's blade against the deadbolt first and pressed the trigger. It screamed through the steel one millimeter at a time, spraying a jet of golden sparks against the doorframe. Then he moved on to the padlock.

A few more seconds of the piercing noise and the U-shaped shackle was cut all the way through. Deputy Rickard lifted the lock from the bolt and placed it in an evidence bag. Then he opened the door.

The stairway was dark, but there was a light on at the bottom. Manuel's heart began to pound. He turned on his flashlight. When deputies Rickard and Hale saw him draw his gun, they drew theirs too. Manuel led them down the stairs.

"Wayne County Sheriff's Department," he called out. His voice echoed in a strange way. Probably something to do with the weird-looking panels all over the walls. The sight of them made him even more anxious. "If there's anyone down here, announce yourself."

No one responded, but there was a flutter of movement on the couch. That's when Manuel noticed the back of someone's head poking above the cushion. They had tight black curls and light black skin.

It can't be, he thought. Because cases like this one never ended this way. But none of the other missing persons were Black. And those curls—longer than he had ever seen Zion grow them—looked just like his mother's. Manuel holstered his handgun and practically flew the rest of the way down the stairs.

He called out again as he hurried toward the couch. But the person—Zion, it had to be—never turned around. Didn't move a muscle even when Manuel came to a stop right in front of him.

It was indeed his nephew. And he was alive. Not alive and well, though, it seemed. The boy had a thousand-yard stare that was fixed unblinking on the basement wall. From the corner of his bottom lip, a strand of drool dangled and threatened to fall at any moment.

Shock is what it was. Manuel had seen it before. One time he'd arrived at the scene of a nasty collision to see a mother limping down the highway holding her daughter's severed leg in her arms. When he caught up to her, she'd looked just like Zion looked now.

"What did she do to you, kid?" Manuel asked, knowing he wouldn't answer. Then, into his radio, "This is Garcia. I need an EMT at 100 Hawkins Road."

"Copy that," the dispatcher said.

"Help me with him," Manuel said to the deputies standing on either side of him. "Let's get him out of here."

He looped his arm under Zion's shoulder and started to lift, but Deputy Hale stopped him.

"Sheriff, wait," she said. "Look."

Manuel looked at where she was pointing and noticed for the first time the shackle around Zion's ankle and the chain bolted to the cinderblock wall.

"That evil bitch," he muttered. Then, louder, "We still got that grinder?"

"I left it upstairs," Deputy Rickard said.

"Go get it."

"Yes, sir."

Manuel knelt in front of his nephew and put his hand on his knee. "Look at me, Zion," he said, then continued anyway when Zion's eyes never moved. "You're safe now. You're gonna go home."

The strand of saliva hanging from his lip finally fell, splashing against the cement floor. His breath came out a low moan. Like a dying person's last gasp.

"Rickard!" Manuel shouted. "Hurry up!"

"I'm right—"

Here. But he didn't get that part out. Not before the sound of gunshots somewhere in the house sucked the air from the room.

What the hell is happening? Manuel thought. Hale and Rickard were already running up the stairs. Manuel scrambled to his feet, drew his gun, and followed them.

41

Deputy Fred Rodgers had often lamented the lack of excitement in his career. He knew there were perks to being a cop in a small, peaceful town like Hooper Valley. His wife sure slept easier at night knowing he wasn't likely to encounter anything crazier than a reckless driver or teens drinking malt liquor. But sometimes he wished he had at least one good story to tell.

This right here had all the makings of one, though. Charlotte Mallory, the hotshot author, faking her own kid's disappearance. Not only that, the sheriff had them looking for any evidence that would link her to those missing persons cases too. He didn't really get into why, but he seemed pretty sure about it.

It wasn't exactly a chance to prove himself in the heat of action, but it would it least be a good story. Heck, he might even end up on the national news. They probably wouldn't want to interview some random deputy, but he might show up in the background or the B-roll footage.

"Let's check the master bedroom first," Deputy Reed said once they reached the top of the stairs, motioning to an open door at the end of the hallway. Through it, Fred could see the corner of a mattress with a purple comforter over it. "Remember, don't touch anything."

"You ain't got to tell me that," Deputy Rodgers said. Trent Reed was always trying to tell him what do, even though Fred had been at the department longer than he had. He thought because he used to work for Dallas PD, it made him some kind of badass.

"I'll check out the closet," Deputy Reed said. "You check the dresser."

Deputy Rodgers turned on his flashlight and opened the top drawer of the large wooden dresser near the bed. Folded t-shirts were all that was in there. They'd been instructed to look for things like wallets or cell phones. Things Charlotte Mallory might have kept as souvenirs. But Fred figured anyone smart enough to evade capture this long probably would've destroyed all that by now. If anyone was going to find something, his bet was on the cadaver dogs sniffing around outside.

He opened the second drawer and found it full of undergarments. He pilfered through them with the end of his flashlight, but there was nothing hidden underneath them. He started to open the next one when Deputy Reed spoke up.

"You hear that?"

Deputy Rodgers listened. Then he heard it too. The creak of bedsprings, coming from one of the rooms down the hall.

They both stepped out of the master bedroom. Deputy Rodgers put his hand on the butt of his gun, but he kept it holstered; it was probably the kid, and he didn't want to scare him if that was the case.

"Which one you think it came from?" Deputy Reed whispered.

Then, before Fred could say he wasn't sure, they heard the bed creak again. This time, it was clear which room it came from.

They both walked slowly toward the door with a sense of caution neither of them could have really explained. Deputy Rodgers kept his hand clenched around his gun.

"Sheriff's department," Deputy Reed said, leaning against the doorframe. "We're coming in." He turned the knob and pushed open the door.

"Shit!" he shouted, and they both took a couple stumbling steps back. Someone was standing right in front of the door. Staring straight at them like he'd been waiting on them to open it. And the longer Deputy Rodgers stared back, the more his skin began to crawl.

It was the kid they were looking for. Malachi Mallory. His face and hair looked just like the pictures they'd been shown. Except he was a full head taller than Deputy Rodgers now—maybe even taller than Deputy Reed. And the way the boy looked at them scared him more than he could have ever expected.

"Hey, kid," Deputy Reed said. His voice shook just a little. Hearing that made Deputy Rodgers's urge to beat feet away from there even stronger. "Won't you come with us?"

"Who are you?" Malachi said. There was no fear in his voice. A little confusion maybe, but mostly a tone of distrust and anger that matched the glare of his dark eyes.

"We're the police," Deputy Reed said. Somewhere in the back of his mind, Fred Rodgers wondered how he could even speak with those eyes looking at him. To Fred, it felt like he was slipping into them. Like they were whirlpools pulling him in.

Deputy Reed took a step forward. "Let's go," he said. He placed a hand on Malachi's shoulder, then…

Then nothing. Seconds passed while Deputy Reed stood there frozen like a statue. Deputy Rodgers's swirling vision started to clear now that the kid wasn't looking at him anymore. It felt like slowly waking up from a fever dream or coming out of a stupor. The kid's eyes were locked on Deputy Reed now. Deputy Rodgers heard whispers even though Malachi's lips never moved.

"What's happen…" Rodgers started, but both this and the step forward he took were cut short when Deputy Reed sharply turned around.

He staggered a little. Blinked rapidly and struggled to swallow while Deputy Rodgers watched him with a look of stupefied confusion. Then he reached a quivering hand for the gun on his belt.

"Trent, what are you doing, man?" Deputy Rodgers asked.

The gun slid from its holster, shaking so badly in Deputy Reed's hand it was a wonder he held on to it. But when he raised the gun and pointed it at Fred's chest, the shaking suddenly stopped.

"Trent!"

Even as he stared down its barrel, Fred never expected the gun to go off. Trent Reed might be an asshole sometimes, but…

A flower of fire bloomed from the gun before Fred could finish the thought. The explosion in the confined hallway hammered his eardrums at the same instant the slug impacted his chest. It felt just like a hard punch—less painful than he had always imagined but so stunning in these circumstances that shock overtook him at once. He put a hand to the spurting hole, lifted it, and stared at the blood dripping from his fingers like it wasn't real. Then he felt his legs go weak and collapsed to the floor.

Deputy Reed shuffled forward. He was shaking again. Shaking his head back and forth now, too, like a rabid dog. He mumbled something, or maybe it was just a moan; Rodgers's ears were ringing so loudly it was hard to hear anything else. And, already, the world was starting to fade.

Nothing about what he saw made sense anyway. Maybe it was better if he just closed his eyes. Maybe it was just a bad dream he'd wake from if he did.

The vision of Deputy Reed standing over him slowly swirled and faded. The gun, still shaking in his hand but pointed down at Fred's face now, was all that Fred could focus on.

When it fired four rapid shots, he didn't register them at all. The first one cut the lights before his nerves could send a single pain signal.

He never saw the tears begin to stream from Deputy Reed's blue eyes. Nor the way he struggled against his own body's betrayal as he pressed the gun underneath his chin. Only the boy saw this, his own eyes gleaming and his lips stretched into a grin.

Boom, Malachi whispered without speaking.

Unable to resist, Deputy Reed obeyed the command.

<h1 style="text-align:center">4 2</h1>

Manuel couldn't remember the last time he moved so fast. He was a little surprised he still had it in him. He flew up the basement stairs, then tore down the hallway. If the initial gunshots were all he had to go on, he wouldn't have known where in the house they'd come from. But the gunfire had started up again. There were shouts and screams now too. All coming from the home's second story.

He rounded into the living room and looked down the sights of his Glock at the stairwell on the other side. Deputies Hale and Rickard were already halfway up it. Manuel pushed himself even harder to catch up.

From the corner of his eye, he saw something drip from the banister—thick and bright red. But he didn't stop. He caught up with his deputies at the top of the stairway and stacked up with them. Then they all three turned the corner together.

What they saw on the other side of the wall was a scene of unhinged carnage. Blood painted the floor and walls and ceiling in great, dripping swathes. A severed arm leaned against one of the bedroom doors. A bird's nest of entrails sat on the floor just in front of Manuel's boot.

At the end of the gore-littered hall, only one officer was left standing. Manuel couldn't tell who it was from behind, but the person standing in front of the officer was one he recognized—even with his face stained red. It was Charlotte's missing boy. Some impossible, nightmare version of him, but him.

Manuel would have fired without a warning, but the unknown officer stood in the way. Just stood there doing nothing with his hands at his side.

"Get down!" Manuel shouted. Neither he nor the boy listened.

Manuel watched the boy reach out a slender arm. He placed his hand around the officer's throat. Then, in a blurred flash of movement, he ripped it out. Blood sprayed the ceiling as the officer fell backward. His windpipe dangled from Malachi's hand like a gory piece of plastic tubing. What happened next shocked Manuel more than anything he'd witnessed so far. He watched the boy lift the flesh and cartilage to his lips, then slurp them down in one gulp.

Manuel, Deputy Hale, and Deputy Rickard all opened fire at nearly the same instant. But by the time the first muzzle flashed, Malachi was already gone. He'd moved so quickly, Manuel couldn't even tell which room he'd dipped into.

They ceased fire. Silence save for the ringing in Manuel's ears fell over the hallway. The smell of blood and gunpowder and punctured entrails filled his nose.

"Hold your position," he said. "Hale, you radio for backup. Tell them to get every officer they can here."

Surely someone had done that already. But with how fast everything had happened, Manuel couldn't be certain.

Deputy Hale fumbled at her radio, breathing rapidly. Standing beside her, Deputy Rickard looked even worse. All the color had drained from his skin, and his hands trembled wildly as he kept his gun extended.

"Dispatch this is Unit 14," Hale said. "Requesting immediate backup at 100 Hawkins Road. Multiple officers down. Suspect is—"

A loud crash snatched her attention away. It came from the room on the left side at the end of the hallway.

"What was that?" Deputy Rickard said. He sounded on the verge of hysterics.

There was another booming crash. Closer this time—from the room just beside where they stood. It shook the hallway, the distinct crack of splitting boards and plaster clearer now than last time.

He's going through the walls, Manuel realized.

But he realized it a moment too late. Another crash came from directly behind them, this one the loudest yet. An eruption of splinters and drywall exploded into the hallway.

Manuel whirled around just in time to see a blur of movement coming toward them. Deputy Rickard turned around only halfway before the boy impacted him. His feet left the ground, and he soared through the air like he'd just been hit by a truck. Instantly, Malachi was on top of him.

Manuel aimed and fired despite not having a clear shot; Rickard was dead either way if he didn't. At least one of the rounds appeared to find their target, striking the boy (or whatever the hell he was) in the back just above the hip. Manuel saw his shirt ripple, and a spray of blood from the exit wound painted the floor. But Malachi didn't even seem to notice.

A chilling scream filled the hallway as the boy pressed both his thumbs into Deputy Rickard's eye sockets. He lifted his head a couple feet from the floor, then drove it down again impossibly hard. The hardwood splintered beneath the impact. Deputy Rickard's skull cracked open like a busted watermelon.

Manuel and Deputy Hale both let loose a volley of fire. The signature wet thump of bullets smashing flesh followed most of the retorts. Manuel saw the boy stagger a little as he stood from Deputy Rickard's corpse. He fired two more rounds. Two more ragged holes opened up next to the rest riddling Malachi's back.

Go down, you bastard. Despite all the insanity he'd witnessed, Manuel couldn't believe he hadn't dropped already.

Instead, the boy whirled around and flung his arm over his head like a pitcher throwing a baseball. Manuel had just enough time to identify the object in his hand—Deputy Rickard's service weapon—before it was whizzing through the air.

It sailed end over end and buzzed past the side of Manuel's face close enough for him to feel the breeze on his skin. For an instant, he thought the boy had missed. Then he heard the sound of Deputy Hale's knees striking the ground.

He turned around, taking his eyes off their attacker for a dangerous instant, to see Hale crawling on all fours. Blood poured in buckets from where the butt of the gun had caved in her forehead, splitting skin and bone. She dragged herself forward another foot, then slumped to her stomach.

There'd be time for grief and anger. Time for terror, too, if he lived to see all the sleepless nights that would surely follow this day. But for now, all Manuel felt was a silent calm.

The gun in his hand was empty, its slide locked back. His other hand dropped to the spare magazine on his belt, and he slid it from its pouch in a *mostly* smooth motion; he must have practiced no telling how many thousands of speed reloads over the years, but it's a different beast when your life is on the line.

Malachi's eyes darted to the gun. He watched the empty magazine fall from its grip when Manuel hit the release button. Then, just as Manuel slammed the new mag into place, Malachi shot forward.

He moved slower than before. Maybe all those hollow points he'd eaten had done something after all, Manuel thought. But it was still going to be too late. By the time he chambered a round, the monster was already on him.

Manuel hit the floor hard enough to drive the air from his chest. He tried to sit up immediately, but Malachi pinned him down. The pressure against Manuel's shoulders as the boy pushed them down was crushing. He heard one of them pop, and the pain set off sparks in his vision.

Malachi leaned forward until his face was inches from Manuel's, then let loose an ear-splitting scream. Blood dripped from his gaping mouth. It pooled in his eyes so that the whites of them were streaked red. Just as Manuel began to raise the gun he'd managed to keep hold of, those eyes froze every muscle in his body.

A splitting pain tore through his head, like claws digging into his skull, but Manuel couldn't even wince. Not a muscle in his body was his to control anymore. He felt the pressure pinning his arms to the floor begin to lift as Malachi relaxed his grip. He commanded his hand over and over to lift the gun and fire. But it just wouldn't move.

Then a voice—growling and disembodied and so loud it felt concussive—filled every corner of his thoughts.

KILL YOURSELF!

Manuel's right arm twitched. The gun lifted an inch off the floor. When he realized it wasn't him doing it, he struggled against his own limb's betrayal with everything he had.

DO IT!

The gun was nearly pointed at the ceiling now. Manuel's arm continued to rise no matter how hard he fought it. And fighting it was getting more and more difficult. The whole world seemed so far away all of a sudden. Like he was already dead and leaving it.

Part of him wanted to embrace this feeling. To stop fighting, go into whatever darkness or light waited for him on the other side. Life had stopped making sense the moment he entered this hallway. Almost every friend he had lay dead around him.

But then Zion crossed his scattered, fading thoughts. He was still chained up in the basement. God knows what they had planned for him.

Manuel had done more good in this life than bad, he liked to think. He could have left it at peace. But he wasn't leaving it until he saved his sister's kid.

The barrel of the Glock 26 he'd carried for the past fourteen years continued its trajectory to the side of his head. Manuel waited. Waited for the fleeting moment its path crossed Malachi's face. Then he summoned every ounce of will to force a single motion.

Manuel's trigger finger twitched. Just enough. Just *barely* enough.

The gun barked. The recoil tore it from his limp hand. In an instant, the trance he'd been frozen within evaporated.

Malachi continued to stare down at him at first, but the bewitchment was gone from his eyes. Just below his right eye, a quarter-sized entry wound leaked blood, its rim framed by splinters of bone. Manuel sat up and shoved the boy off him. He fell to the side and didn't move.

Manuel staggered at first—the numbness still leaving his limbs—and had to catch himself on the stair rails. But he quickly found his footing again. Everything moved in a blur as he raced back to the basement. His thoughts most of all.

For now, the only thought that mattered was getting Zion out of here. He'd been right all along about this place; it was cursed. Cursed in ways he'd probably spend the rest of his life trying to comprehend. Every second he spent here, every second his nephew spent chained in that basement, was a second too long.

He couldn't see Zion from the top of the basement stairs when he reached them, but the kid was down there somewhere. Between the shackle and chain and thick bolts in the wall, someone had gone to great lengths to keep him there. Manuel thought of Charlotte, her whereabouts still unknown, and gritted his teeth. He'd see that woman in chains of her own if it was the last thing he ever accomplished as sheriff.

He sprinted down the stairs, then scanned the room for Zion. He spotted him to the right, standing near the far corner of the basement next to the hot water heater. Standing farther away than the chain should have allowed. Then Manuel noticed the grinder hanging from his hand. Deputy Rickard must have dropped it within his reach, and Zion had set himself free.

He still had that empty look about him, though. Like he wasn't really seeing what his eyes were pointed at. Manuel wondered if he might have to carry the boy out of here, then wondered if he even could.

"Let's go home, kid." Manuel reached out his hand and started forward. Zion's eyes shifted to watch him approach, but there was still no sign of any recognition in them.

A sudden noise made Manuel flinch: the gritty whine of a saw blade spinning up to speed. The grinder still hung from Zion's limp arm, but his finger was holding the trigger all the way down.

"Zion, turn that thing—"

Zion charged. Manuel watched him come, stunned at what he was seeing. Reflexively, he raised the gun still clenched in his hand. He centered the tritium sights on his nephew's chest. Purely out of training and survival instinct, he almost pulled the trigger.

Instead, Manuel shut his eyes.

It was time to call it quits. On this day, on whatever ungodly thing that was happening here, on this entire messed up life. He no longer had the will to see it through. Certainly not if it meant gunning down his own flesh and blood.

The scream of the grinder reached a fever pitch. Manuel felt a flash of the brightest pain as its blade tore across his neck. And then it all just leaked away. By the time his knees hit the cement of Charlotte Mallory's basement floor, he was already gone.

267

<h1 style="text-align:center">43</h1>

Despite her heels and skintight jeans, Charlotte ran faster than she had ever run before. All the lights flashing blue and red blew past in a fuzzy glow.

The door to the house was open, and Charlotte barged through it. She saw the first body right there at the entrance to her living room—almost tripped over it—but paid it no mind other than the sinking despair in her chest.

"Malachi!" she screamed. When he didn't answer, that sinking feeling reached a nauseating intensity.

Charlotte sprinted across the living room to the stairs. She passed the hallway and saw the door to the basement wide open on her way there, but she didn't stop. It didn't matter. Not right now.

At the top of the stairs, however, she couldn't help but stop and gasp. There were so many bodies cluttering the hallway, they were stacked on top of one another. The walls were destroyed, peppered with bullet holes. One sported a hole large enough for her to see the toilet and shower on its other side.

The floor was covered with a lake of blood and islands of torn flesh. Charlotte did her best to avoid stepping on the remains as she made her way to Malachi's bedroom, but sometimes there was nowhere else to step. With most mangled beyond recognition, the corpses all looked the same. They all wore the same tan uniform of the Wayne County Sheriff's Department.

All except for one.

Charlotte spotted the blue and yellow striped T-shirt out of the corner of her eye. The tears came at the same time as her scream. She stumbled over the bodies to get to her son and flung herself at where he lay on the floor.

Wounds riddled Malachi's body. One punched a hole through the center of his face—large enough for Charlotte to see the ruined brain matter on the other side.

He was breathing, though. Weakly—so weakly she had to put her face to his nose to be sure—but breathing.

Charlotte's mind raced. An emergency room. That was the only thing she could think of. But then what? What would happen even if they saved him?

Watching the blood still seep from his wounds, sitting there doing nothing, she decided it didn't matter. She looped his arm around her shoulder and lifted with her knees. But she couldn't get him up into the air. She'd heard so many stories of mothers exhibiting superhuman strength when their children's lives were in peril. For her, such superpowers were nowhere to be found.

"I'm so sorry, baby," she wept. Then she took him by the wrists and began dragging him down the hall.

A vehicle was the next challenge. Hers was still parked at some bar whose name she'd already forgotten. There were plenty of them parked outside, though. She stopped and let go of Malachi's wrists, reached into the pocket of a headless corpse near her feet, and pulled out a pair of keys.

She put them between her teeth, then grabbed hold of Malachi again, wincing at the way his body bumped and jostled as she pulled him down the stairs.

Once they were out the front door, getting him down the concrete steps of her porch was even more distressing, and she lifted with all the strength in her arms to keep his head from touching the ground.

The sound of her sobs and gravel sliding beneath her son's back filled the night air. In the moonlight and flashing strobes, she noticed the trail of crimson he'd left in the dirt.

With a shaking hand, she pressed the center button on the key fob she'd taken. Headlights flashed on a squad car parked on the grass near her flower bed, and its horn beeped once.

It took everything she had to get Malachi into the passenger seat. She might have pulled a muscle in her back, but the pain was such a distant concern, it would be much later before she knew. She didn't bother with sitting him up or trying to buckle him in. She just slammed the door and hurried around to the driver's side.

Charlotte swiped her fingers all over the car's foreign dash until she found the push-start button. The engine purred, and she threw the car into drive.

Evergreen Memorial Hospital was the closest one. Not the best by any means, but closest was much more important. She tore down her gravel driveway so fast the car's traction control light blinked at her as the tires spun out.

The highway came into view. Left was where she needed to turn—into town—and Charlotte didn't bother with the blinker. Or stopping either for that matter. But the second she started to spin the wheel, a voice froze her.

Not the hospital.

It came from nowhere, in that same, awful way Malachi had spoken to her before. But it was not Malachi's voice. It was a voice she'd last heard years ago, and yet she recognized it immediately.

She hit the accelerator again and turned the car to the left anyway.

Turn around, the voice said. Like a damn GPS she couldn't shut off. Charlotte screamed between gritted teeth and sped up even faster.

You know what they'll do to him.

This was the first thing he said that really got her attention. Because it was true. She'd pictured it clearly a thousand times before—what would happen if the powers of this world discovered her son. Tears clouded Charlotte's vision, making it hard to see the road ahead. She wiped her eyes with the back of her hand, then glanced at Malachi in the passenger seat. Still motionless. Still seeping blood.

"He's going to die anyway!" she screamed at the windshield.

He won't.

It seemed like a foolish thing to be so sure about. But he *was* still alive when anyone else would have been dead ten times over; Charlotte could see his chest still feebly rising and falling. Fingers of doubt crept in. Her muscles buzzed with indecision.

Turn around, and I'll get you somewhere safe.

Charlotte let out another scream. She smashed her hands into the steering wheel as she drove, honking the car's horn sporadically. What good had ever come from listening to this man? Whatever good there had been, had it ever been worth it in the end?

I won't let him die, Charlotte. His fate has not yet been fulfilled.

A flash of movement in the rearview mirror caught her eye. Perhaps just a shadow from the moonlight and the trees passing by. But then she saw in the glass a set of dimly glowing eyes, and she felt his presence there with them.

A coldness filled the car, prickling her skin. A smothering darkness stemmed from the back seat, and she wondered briefly how on earth she'd missed it the first time, all those years ago. Missed the blackness of this thing's soul. Missed the dangers he hardly tried to hide.

It hadn't mattered to her then. That was the only explanation. Just like it didn't matter now. She believed what he'd said; whoever he was, whatever his aims, Malachi would live if his father wanted him to.

Time slowed. Then, finally, so did she—just enough to swerve the wheel without sending them into the ditch and safely turn the car around.

4 4

Out the window of her cottage, Charlotte watched the wind whip sheets of snow through the Siberian pines. There was a time she would have called such arctic conditions a blizzard—the storm of the century. But, in this desolate corner of the globe, it was just another autumn afternoon.

There was a time, too, when a thought like this might have made her smile. But joy was a shadow these days: faint, fleeting, always gone by the time the sun went down. And today, what she saw out the window ripped any remnants of it away long before the sunset.

It wasn't the weather. She was used to that already, and winter would bring much worse. But more than snow drifted through the trees outside her cottage. More than a storm approached.

The figure trudged through the sparse forest, still too far away for her to see anything but their silhouette. They could have been a man or woman, young or old. Hopefully not a child—and they did at least appear too tall for this to be the case. Charlotte wasn't sure she could live with it being a child again. Though, truthfully, that was just a lie she told herself. She'd live with whatever she had to. Just like always.

The visitors who journeyed on foot through the tundra to her isolated home came on a near weekly basis now. And never of their own accord. Some walked dozens of miles from the villages to the south and west. Some were so badly frostbitten and fatigued by the time they arrived, they seemed to embrace their death.

It was Malachi who brought them here. Whispered to them from across the wilderness and commanded them to come. Charlotte had tried to imagine what it must be like for them, lying in bed, tending to whatever chores occupied their days, then hearing his voice in their heads. Like the call of the void, impossible to resist.

Her days of hunting for him had ended the moment the two of them arrived here. Not once since then had she even left the place. There'd been no reason to; the visitors Malachi summoned always brought with them everything she needed—food, medicine, sometimes little trinkets or things he must have thought pretty. Malachi hardly spoke anymore, rarely even showed the slightest touch of emotion. His commitment to providing for her like she had once done for him was the only way she knew that he still loved her.

Yet it wasn't the gifts the person might be bearing that Charlotte thought of as she watched the figure approach. It never was. The deepest guilt was all she ever felt. It ripped and gnawed at her like hungry rats with every step closer the figure out her window took toward their impending doom.

They were coming into view now. It appeared to be a man—someone tall and well-built. Well-dressed too. Thick parkas and sheepskin coats were the attire most villagers in this area wore. But the man trudging through the snow wore solid black. A suit, it seemed. Charlotte felt her heart begin to pound.

She turned away from the window, not bothering to put on a coat of her own or even her boots, and opened the cottage's single door. A blast of arctic wind stung her skin. What she saw chilled her much more.

She'd always known this day would come. One would think that thirteen years of bracing for it might make it easier. But when she saw his face again and his eyes shining like onyx against the solid white surroundings, panic seized her.

She took off through the snow, running toward him without any kind of plan. She could cry and beg, drape herself around him and make him drag her. It wouldn't do any good, but she was compelled to try.

The man—the father of her son—watched her come. Charlotte could feel his eyes tearing into her. He kept walking at the same, unbothered pace. He only stopped when Charlotte was right in front of him, standing in his way.

His face looked the same as it had the night they met. Not a single wrinkle of difference, while her hair was gray and her features had aged much more than thirteen years should have inflicted.

"Move, Charlotte," he said, his deep voice carrying over the whipping wind.

"No," Charlotte said, despite knowing he could kill her with a look.

"You won't stop this. No one will."

Behind her, Charlotte heard the cottage door opening. Her heart sank even lower. Heavy footsteps crunched through the tightly packed snow. A shadow enveloped her as Malachi strolled up behind her.

She watched the man's eyes lift to take him in. A teenager as of last month, their son now stood almost nine feet tall. Muscles like mooring ropes lined his lean body. His boyish features were all but gone, slowly replaced over the last few years by features more angular and defined.

A few more thudding footsteps and he stood beside her. Wind lifted the hems of the furs Charlotte had sewn herself into a coat as large as a blanket. Malachi stared curiously at the phantom in front of them, his wolflike eyes unblinking.

"Hello, Abaddon," his father spoke. Charlotte flinched at that name.

Malachi—because that was his name and always would be to her—didn't answer. And Charlotte felt a glimmer of hope.

"Come with me, Abaddon. There is—"

"Who are you?" Charlotte interjected. "...*what* are you?" If nothing else, no matter what happened here, she needed to know.

The man, or phantom, or Devil himself perhaps, regarded her with a look of thin patience. "Someone not of this world," he finally replied.

"What the hell is that supposed to mean?" Charlotte spat. She could tell by the way he looked away from her that he had no intention of answering.

"It's time," he said to Malachi. He reached out his hand. Deep down, Charlotte knew what would happen if Malachi took it. In a blink, they'd both be gone, and she'd be left standing there alone in the forest. Never to see her son again.

"Malachi, don't!" she said. Then, turning wet, angry eyes back to his father, "What do you want with him?"

This brought a touch of a terrible smile to the man's face—brought a flash of the fire she'd glimpsed before to his eyes. "Your world is ending, Charlotte. Ending very soon. The child you bore, raised...fed...he is the catalyst of its destruction."

She saw it then: a vision forming amidst the falling snow. Colors and shapes coming together just as they had in this man's bedroom thirteen years ago, when he showed her the future he offered.

Part of the future he offered.

This time, she saw cities burning. Armies of men and women like locusts in a swarm, all dead eyed and dead inside. All rising up to follow her son's command.

Yet despite how horrible it all was, she realized she didn't care. Malachi leaving her was still the only part that tortured her. Even the thought of the whole world burning didn't frighten her nearly as much as the thought of dying alone in this wilderness.

The man's smile was beaming now. He looked on the verge of laughter. "There you are, Charlotte. There's the girl I chose. You really would do anything for him, wouldn't you? *Anything*. And not because you love him. No, that's only half of it. It's because he's the only one in the whole wide world who loves *you*."

"Please," Charlotte said. It was all she had left.

"Take my hand, Abaddon."

Charlotte started to step in front of him, but Malachi gently pushed her aside. Her heart sank as he stepped forward.

"That's not my name," he said, stopping in front of his father. Ignoring his outstretched hand.

The words caught Charlotte by surprise. Through tear-blurred eyes, she anxiously watched for his father's reaction. But not a spark of emotion slipped through his intense gaze.

"It is," the man said. "It always has been. And when the last of mankind lie waiting for the end, Abaddon will be the name on their dying breaths."

"No," Malachi said. "I'm not going with you."

Charlotte felt like laughing. Crying. Screaming at the top of her lungs all at the same time. But she kept her lips sealed, not daring jeopardize what was unfolding.

Malachi and his father fixed each other in a frozen stare. Like whispers on the wind, Charlotte could almost make out the unspoken conversation taking place between them. The intensity of it charged the air so heavily she could feel the static on her skin even more clearly than the stinging cold.

She held her breath. Then, at last, it ceased. A silent calm settled over the woods.

The phantom in front of her broke his stare with Malachi and fixed it on Charlotte. The rage in his dark eyes both elated and terrified her.

"This is not over," he said. His voice was steady, smooth as always, yet dripping with acid. "He will change his mind one day. Fate will call to him every minute. One day, he's going to answer."

"Then I guess I'll see you then." The smugness could have gotten her killed, she realized. But if he killed her, Malachi would never accept him. Because he was right about one thing: her son did love her.

Without any parting remark or final look of contempt, the man was gone. Vanished on a puff of wind like a candle flame blown out.

For a moment, Charlotte stood there and watched the place where he had been. Watched the snowflakes swirling in the empty air. Then she took Malachi by the hand and walked with him back to the cottage.

4 5

Zion leaned over the balcony of his sixth-story apartment and watched the city wake up. There'd been times over the years when the thought of jumping from this spot had flashed across his mind. But he'd never given up before and didn't plan to start.

It was just past 6:30 in the morning. The city lights to the west still outshone the tangerine glow to the east. A few bright stars still spotted the indigo sky.

He was up earlier than any of the roommates he shared the place with. Up earlier than most everyone on a Saturday morning. But he never went back to sleep when he woke from a nightmare, no matter what time of night it was; the risk of slipping right back into the same dream was too high, he'd found. Most of the time—weather permitting—he came out here.

At least the nightmares were happening less and less often, it seemed. That's how his therapist had said it would go. Zion hadn't believed her at first—there was a time when imagining anything ever getting better defied all reason—but what do you know, she'd been right.

She'd also said there'd be closure someday, though, and so far, that was not true. How could he ever have closure when all anyone wanted was to sweep what happened to him under the rug? Thirteen dead cops—some torn apart, some shot with their own guns—was something the suits who'd descended on Hooper Valley could not begin to explain. And Zion, the event's sole survivor, hadn't been much help. It had taken nearly three months before he spoke a single word. By then, his memory of it all was an opaque fog.

Accepting that he'd never know what happened to him in that house during that lost year of his life—or what happened to his uncle and friends and all the rest who died—was the hardest part. In his nightmares, he invented a thousand possible explanations. In the daytime, he wondered which one, if any of them, was true.

He might not know the truth, but he could feel it still. It was buried deep, deeper than he could ever hope to reach, but still detectable at times when the world was quiet and his thoughts completely still. Sometimes it felt like a void within him. A part of him that had been erased. Taken away. Other times it felt just the opposite: like something that shouldn't be there. Remnants of a malignance left behind.

He couldn't shake it and had stopped trying. But he'd not stopped trying when it came to all the rest. He had a job now. Not as an economist like he'd once aspired to (going back to school just wasn't in the cards for him anymore), but he enjoyed working at the golf course as much as anyone can expect to enjoy their job. He saw his mom and dad at least once a week. He had friends. Women, too, when he wanted them, though the idea of holding down a relationship with one was still too much to aim for right now.

Life went on. As long as he kept getting out of bed, going through the motions, so would he. He'd live and someday die not knowing what any of it meant. But that was true for everyone, he supposed. Either way, it would have to be enough.

A gust of chilly wind brought goosebumps to his exposed skin. It was nearing October now, and he was wearing only a T-shirt. He glanced behind him at the glass door to the apartment, thought how a cup of hot coffee might hit the spot on a morning like this, and decided to go in.

Zion rose from the metal chair where he sat and started to turn away from the balcony. Then the sight of something baffling froze him in place.

It looked like the sunrise at first, but to the west instead of the east. And rising far too rapidly. It engulfed the Dallas skyline in a brilliant fireball, quickly growing so intense that it burned his eyes, and he had to look away.

The shockwave hit him just as he turned his head. It shook the railing of the balcony. Shattered the glass behind him and shattered his eardrums just as completely. In an instant, the whole world went silent. Zion staggered and had to catch himself against the balcony.

As he watched the cloud of fire and debris rising into the twilight sky, ears that would hear nothing else ever again heard a voice he knew well from his nightmares.

Come, it commanded, loud and undeniable.

Like all the rest who heard this call, Zion obeyed.

T H E   E N D

The Dark Thing

A psychological/supernatural horror novel

The son of a schizophrenic, Jared Gordon has lived his entire life with a genetic time bomb coded into his DNA. So when the night terrors and hallucinations arrive in force, it seems undeniable that the same disease responsible for his father's suicide is to blame.

But a bizarre reunion with his estranged brother and a journal from their father resurface chilling childhood memories that cast his current experiences in a sinister new light. To have any hope of salvation, Jared must find proof whether the nightmare he's living is a descent into madness or an assault from a supernatural force more ancient and evil than Hell itself. Yet at every turn, the answer only grows more impossible to believe, upending his view of himself, his past, and the very nature of reality.

Worst of all is the growing suspicion that his youngest daughter Elena – an eccentric little girl prone to strange and sometimes unsettling behaviors – may be responsible for setting into motion a cataclysm that began decades before she was born.

JOHN ASHLEY is a freelance writer and indie author who lives in Springfield, Missouri. What started as a love for ghost stories and Goosebumps books turned into a lifelong passion for all things horror, and writing horror books is the bloody, beating heart of that passion. When he's not writing, John enjoys watching sports, spending time outdoors, and hanging out with his wife and their three pets

For updates on new releases and other important news, join John Ashley's newsletter at johnashleyauthor.com.

www.ingramcontent.com/pod-product-compliance
Lightning Source LLC
Chambersburg PA
CBHW020131310726
48970CB00006B/1823